THE *Art*

OF DUST

MEL A ROWE

Also by MEL A ROWE

Winter's Walk

The Football Whisperer

Avoiding the Pity Party

Unplanned Party

The Australian Bestselling
ELSIE CREEK SERIES:

The ART of DUST

DIAMOND in the DUST

CAKED in DUST

XMAS DUST

Visit MelAROWE.com for more

COPYRIGHT

The Following Is Written In Australian English

I consider the ELSIE CREEK SERIES a love letter to the unique individuals that continue to shape the Northern Territory into a truly amazing part of Australia.

My dad would've loved it.

One

It's a strange sensation being weighed down by guilt. It made Kat grip the steering wheel tighter while her internals stirred with the giddy sensation she'd once loved as a child. All from the faded road sign that read, *Welcome to Elsie Creek.*

'Did you live here, Mummy?' Kaytlyn asked, brushing away the auburn strands freeing themselves from her pigtails. Her sparkling, lapis lazuli blue eyes, took in the passing view.

'Only for the summers.'

'When?' Kaytlyn asked, straining her neck to see while her finger marked the page of the colouring book nestled within her purple tutu.

'Before you were born.' Back when life was so much simpler.

'How come you've never told me about this place?'

Kat never wanted to. She didn't even want to make this trip.

'Is that a tractor? And, it's...*moving*.' Kaytlyn waved

energetically at the farmer like he was a famous movie star, driving a slow tractor as they passed him on the road. 'This is the country, isn't it? Like real milk-making country?'

'Not that kind of cow, sweetheart. They're beef cattle.'

Their hire van, with the U-Haul trailer rattling behind them, slowed as they approached the herd spilling over the sides of the road. Men in sweat-stained Akubra's steered their quads around the cattle with horns bigger than the handlebars on their bikes. Stocky Blue and Red Heelers yapped at the Brahman's heels, while more stockmen on horseback whistled as the odd stockwhip crack rang in the air.

'Mum, they're cowboys rounding up the herd!'

'Don't call them that. This is Australia and they're cattlemen, stockmen, ringers or drovers, and they're mustering the mob or they're droving. *I think*—it's been a while.'

She drove through the herd and continued along the open highway that stretched like a never-ending black carpet. It sliced through the centre of red dirt scrublands, with the railway line running alongside. All heading for the tiny Northern Territory town, dead ahead.

They passed rolling fields of drying grass waving in the breeze like a huge green sea. Tall gum trees crested hills that kissed the cerulean skyline where wallabies lazed in their shade. Nestled amongst its bark-peeling branches were flocks of white cockatoos, hiding from the late afternoon sun. The familiar countryside generated an electrical hum beneath Kat's skin. She was glad this long drive was almost over.

Then the hard part would begin.

Again, the weight of dread slammed heavily across her shoulder blades.

'Can't wait to go bushwalking with you, Mummy.' Kaytlyn clicked the heels of her new hiking boots, peeking out from the edge of her tutu.

Kat hadn't hiked in years. 'Tell me again, please, what are the rules of walking anywhere out here?'

'Always take a hat, a water bottle, sunscreen, snacks for the trail, and tell someone where you're going. Carry a big stick to smack the ground to scare snakes and goannas getting suntans across the tracks. Don't use the stick to poke down holes, coz the scorpions and spiders can kill you. Don't climb trees that don't have green ants on 'em coz they'll have white ants that eat trees inside out, so they'll break. Don't play near fruit bats coz they can make you very, very sick. Don't pat the cattle coz of their horns…um, am I missing something?'

'Water. What did I tell you about the water? It's the most important,'—*and terrifying*— 'part.'

'Oh, I'm never ever allowed to go swimming in any of the water holes, billabongs, rivers, lakes, streams or seas, and I have to stay back from the water's edge coz the man-eating crocodiles like to eat children for lunch.'

The place didn't sound like fun at all. 'Are you okay with all that?' Kat wasn't.

'I can't wait. How come you know all this when you

grew up in the city, like me?' Kaytlyn sat taller, her fingertips reaching for the dashboard, causing her crayons to spill out of her tutu and onto the floor of their rental van.

'I used to stay with Uncle Frank and Aunty Bea for school holidays.' A time she once lived for.

'Bee, like a black and yellow stripy bee that stings? I can spell that—B.E.E.'

'Brilliant. Although, the native bees here don't sting, but the wasps do.' Was there anything good she could share without scaring her daughter back to the more civilized southern states of Australia. 'Oh, and you spell Aunty Bea, B.E.A. It's short for Beatrice.'

Kaytlyn sat back mouthing the letters, committing the new spelling word to her fast-growing vocabulary. 'How come they don't visit us?'

'How many days has it taken us to get here?'

'Five. It's the longest road trip of my life!'

Kat laughed at the seriousness of the six-year-old wearing a tutu and hiking boots.

'Do Aunty Bea and Uncle...' Kaytlyn waved her crayon like a wand.

'Frank, short for Franklin.' Everyone's name was shortened, including her own of Kathryn to Kat.

'Yeah, him. Do they have any children I can play with?'

'No.' *They would've loved some.* 'I'm sure there are plenty of new friends to make in your new school, honey.' Kat hoped she sounded excited when she'd rather be back in their studio apartment. All this space was daunting compared to the comforting claustrophobic cocoon of a capital city.

She sat higher behind the steering wheel as they entered the town's main street, with its row of shops on either side. There was the hardware-feedstore, the small supermarket, and the mighty pub that stood proud as the centre of this small country town. There was a park with signs pointing to the train station's Tea Room.

Even though she hadn't seen the place in seven years, the town was the same, as if stuck in some weird time warp, except now it had a set of pedestrian lights guarding a zebra crossing.

'What's that?' Kaytlyn asked, pointing to the road ahead.

Kat slammed on the brakes and stared over the steering wheel with wide eyes. 'I think it's a water buffalo.'

A short, black, shiny-nosed water buffalo stood smack in the middle of the road, in the centre of town. It stared at them through long black lashes, chewing like a cow, with red ribbons waving on the breeze from its curved horns.

Was it going to charge their hire van?

'It's got ribbons on it, Mummy, so it must be someone's pet, huh?'

A ute across the road tooted its horn, and the driver shouted out of his window. '*Get off the road, Cecil.*'

The buffalo kept chewing as he ever so casually strolled in front of Kat's car. Red ribbons waved off its horns and tail, and on its sides were large letters written in bright red chalk.

'What does that writing say, Mummy?'

'Um…Choose your movie for the marathon today.' *Weird.*

As the buffalo ambled along the sidewalk, they continued down the main street in silence. At the outer edge of town, they turned onto a bitumen road, where properties extended into acreage.

A group of children played in the street while push bikes lay in the grass on the side of the road.

Déjà vu hit Kat like she'd woken inside a dream, slowing down for the game of street-cricket where the children stopped and stared as they drove past.

'Mummy, how come they're playing on the road?'

'They do that in the country.' Just like she used to.

'There are more children on this street than in our whole building. Will they all be going to my new school?'

'I assume so.' There was only one local bush school, with the nearest boarding school over four hours away by bus. It was a ride Kat knew well.

They approached the road's dead-end before an expansive field of golden grasses that rippled in the breeze. At the sight of the two-storey weather-worn house, her heart hitched a lump into her throat. 'We're here.'

The U-Haul rattled as they entered the driveway. A clipped patch of vivid green lawn ran to the edge of the thriving flower bed where a colourful variety of daisies waved from well-trimmed stems.

Aunty Bea loved daisies. Every time Kat spotted daisies in the shops, she thought of Aunty Bea. Now here she was, once again, staring at Aunty Bea's daisies as if she'd only been here this morning.

Out of the car, Kat stretched her legs, grateful to be free from the steering wheel. She inhaled the fresh open air with its rich earthy floral aroma, but there were none of the familiar summer scents of fruiting mangoes or rambutans. The rambutan trees she used to climb to collect fruit or cover with bird nets, were now pruned back to mere skeletons, standing like silent soldiers along the side of the driveway.

With her hand shading her eyes, she stared up at the mighty Australian Red Cedar. Its lush canopy and curved branches held elkhorns, bird's nest ferns, and orchids along its sturdy limbs. It stood tall and solid in the front yard, making it an oddity, considering the dry outback surrounds.

Coming from a place of no trees, where the sun played hide and seek amongst solid city buildings, she smiled at the goliath. It was the first tree Uncle Frank planted for Aunty Bea when they got married and built this house.

But it wasn't just the tree that made her smile, because hidden among its wide branches stood a simple wooden structure. It was the fort of many seasons. A place for sleep-outs and hideaways, and a keeper of a little girl's secrets guarded and cherished in the one small place. It was the first dwelling she'd ever decorated—every single summer.

It was the treehouse.

She frowned at the grey, washed-out, sagging wooden floorboards. Sun-faded paint peeled away from its outer walls, and the curtains she'd sewn were now nothing more than rags. The ladder still stood in place along the solid trunk while a rope creaked from the swing hanging from its lower branches.

Did she still have the skills to scale that rope?

The front door burst open, and with reading glasses in one hand, her wide linen trousers fluttered with her long shirt as the woman rushed to greet them. 'You're here!'

'Who's that?' Kaytlyn asked, sliding her tiny hand into Kat's.

Kat's vision blurred as her throat thickened. 'It's Aunty Bea.'

'She looks like a storybook nana.'

'Does she?' Kat tilted her head at Aunty Bea. Although the hair was greyer and there were a few more laugh lines, she still had the same plump red cheeks and wide smile.

'So, you've made it,' cried out Aunty Bea, squeezing Kat in her arms.

'Hi, Aunty.' Kat hugged the smaller woman, inhaling that same warm aroma of vanilla essence and chocolate that was sweet, comforting, and the scents of a home. Until now, she'd never realised why she always chose that blend for her candles—her secret weapon that helped seal her many house deals.

'So, let me look at you,' Aunty Bea said, holding Kat at arms-length. 'Beautiful, as always.'

'Really?' *Did Aunty Bea need to clean her glasses?* Kat smoothed a hand over her messy ponytail, trying to tuck her car-crinkled shirt into her cargo pants. She was in dire need of a hot shower and a decent cup of coffee that didn't come in a takeaway cup. But then again, a compliment was a rare thing— even if Aunty Bea was being polite. 'Thanks.'

'Do I have a ballerina in my yard?' Aunty Bea asked as she bent down to the small child.

'I'm no ballerina—they don't do boots. See?' Kaytlyn clumsily pointed her hiking boot's toe like a ballerina.

'So, you're not a ballerina?' Aunty Bea arched a questioning eyebrow at Kat.

'Kaytlyn had one lesson,' Kat said, holding up her finger. 'Every year she asks to go, but only does *one lesson*. She only attends for the tutus.' Kat shrugged, then twirled her hand with a flourish as she bowed to Kaytlyn, playing her part as the court jester. 'Aunty Bea, please allow me to present to you, the tiara-less, tutu-loving, Princess Kaytlyn.'

Kaytlyn giggled as she gave a clumsy curtsey in her purple tutu, jeans, and hiking boots that had never seen dirt. 'Pleased to meet you.'

'So nice to meet you too, Kaytlyn.' Aunty Bea shook Kaytlyn's hand then pulled her into her arms. 'But we like to hug family when we meet them.'

'I like her, Mummy,' Kaytlyn said, muffled in the hug.

'I like you too, so come along, let's get you inside.'

'You two go ahead, I'll get the bags.' Kat watched Aunty

Bea hold Kaytlyn's hand as they walked along the garden path to the front door. Again, déjà vu sent a chill down her spine that fought against the warmth in her chest. It was soon followed by another pang of guilt hitting heavily across her shoulders, twisting her stomach into a knot.

Where was her sense of adventure, that thrill she experienced as a child whenever she returned to this place of so many happy memories?

If only she could avoid those who hurt her, which was a challenge in a town this small, when she was only here at the request of a dying man.

Two

Kat took a deep, shaky breath as she wiped sweaty palms down her jeans. It was this visit she'd been dreading the most.

She pushed open the door and entered the off-white room, wincing at the sterile scents of disinfectants and floor polish. A large hospital bed stood in the middle of a multitude of gadgets and doo-hickeys that beeped and blipped. At the centre of it all lay a sleeping man.

It couldn't be him. 'Uncle Frank?'

This guy was old, with grey hair and beard. Pale, blue-veined, paper-thin wrinkled skin, puckered around his sunken cheekbones.

Where was her Uncle Frank, the biggest man she ever knew? The man who would scoop her up and sling her over his shoulders, so high she could reach for the sky.

He opened his eyes and blinked at her. 'Kat?'

'Hi, Uncle Frank.' *Can't say how are you, can't say you're looking good,* she didn't know what to say.

'You made it.' He clutched her hand, coughing and wheezing as he tried to sit up.

'Hey, no need to move,' she said, placing her hands on his frail shoulders.

'Let me get a look at you, kiddo,' Frank said with a grin as he slipped on his spectacles.

There he is. She smiled, recognising the grin.

'All grown up, I see.'

'Not that I'm any wiser.' She grimaced, rubbing her palm's heel across her aching chest, her throat too tight to swallow, and her eyes started to water.

Frank chortled as he sat taller, shifting hoses and leads to the pumping machines that surrounded his bed. 'Bein' old and wise is nothin' but a load of bulldust followin' a road-train. Now, did you bring Kaytlyn?'

'She's asleep at Aunty Bea's. I wanted to see you first.' She also wanted to see how bad he was before she brought Kaytlyn to visit.

'Come on, gimme a cuddle, kiddo.' Frank lifted his arms, and she hugged him. Gone were the strong arms and large broad chest, now it was just skin and bone.

A tear escaped to trickle down her cheek. 'I'm sorry.'

'Now, now, it's okay.'

No, it's not. 'I'm sorry I wasn't here sooner.'

'You're here now, that's all that matters,' Uncle Frank said, wiping away her tears. 'You're staying for a while, I hope?'

'Um…'

'Bea's been looking forward to your visit, she'd love the company.'

'We're here.' It was all she could promise.

He squeezed her hand, giving her *the nod* as if he understood.

'Does your daughter suffer from the same artistic decorating obsession as you?'

Kat shared a smile. 'The tiara-less princess is currently working out what she wants to do with her new room at your place.' Her old room was now her daughters, with Kat upgraded to the guest room.

'Home, kiddo,' he said, patting her hand. 'Bea and I have always said to you, it's your home too. It's not a place, so call it *home*.'

'*Home,* then.' It was the same story every trip, but Kat never allowed herself to get attached to places, she just couldn't afford to.

'Still handy with the tools, huh?'

'Well, I was taught by the best.'

'Now what wonderful, handsome, charming man did that?'

She grinned at the handyman she had on speed dial. 'Thank you for answering my questions whenever I called.'

'Did you fix that plumbing problem in the shower?'

'Sure did. You were right about them putting in the wrong fittings for the shower head, and the tape they'd used was worn out.'

'Good, coz the ol' home needs a few repairs.'

'But…' *Surely not.* Only Uncle Frank fixed his home, which he did with the utmost tender care.

'The ol' shed will need a clean-up too. Bea's been rattling around in there, so I reckon it'll be a bit of a dingo's done dinner in there for finding tools.'

'Really?' Bea never went into the shed. *How long had Aunty Bea been dealing with Uncle Frank's cancer on her own?* 'I'll do it.' Kat was all about fixing things, but how big was the workload? 'How come you didn't tell me sooner?'

'We didn't want you to worry.'

She arched her eyebrow at him because that's all she'd done since Uncle Frank's phone call.

'We were waiting to see if the treatments worked.'

'I see.' Uncle Frank never burdened anyone with his troubles, yet he was always first to help anyone in need.

'I knew you needed to finish the kitchen before you could put the place on the market. Did you sell or lease?'

'Lease. I own two apartments in the same building now.' She still got giddy at the thought.

'Really?'

'Ah-huh. It's in a good area, near a great school, with a park across the road. I pretty much signed the lease the day I put it on the market.'

'Clever girl. Maybe you'll find something here in town to keep you busy.'

'We'll see.' Not when she didn't know how long she was staying. 'I'll tackle your pl—' She hesitated at his raised eyebrow. 'I'll tackle *home* first.'

'Good girl. Now, you didn't drag any bloke along with you?'

'Nope.' *As if.* 'I've got Kaytlyn.'

His brow crinkled at her.

She needed no one. 'I've been busy with Kaytlyn, and work's been—'

A man pushed through the door, his white coat flapping like a cape behind him, wearing a baseball cap and a stethoscope slung around his neck. 'Okay then Frank, it's time to check—hello.' He stopped with a half-eaten apple in his hand.

'Doc, meet my niece, Kathryn. She's driven in from upstate, or is that downstate?'

'Interstate.' She swallowed hard at the new guy standing by the end of the bed while her pulse jumped.

'Kat, meet Doctor Mannen.'

'Hi.' She squeaked out, brushing at her messy hair, internally kicking herself for not wearing makeup. To be honest, she hadn't unpacked yet and didn't even know where anything was. She also hadn't wanted to wear smudging mascara while visiting a dying man—in case she cried.

'Stewart, please.' His smile made her toes curl in her boots.

Not good. 'Hi, um, Stewart.' Kat shook his cold hand, so

much softer than her own fingernail-chipped, paint-stained working hands. It would take her a dozen manicures to even get close to the doctor's current standard. It had never bothered her before, until now.

Standing back from the guy, she hid her hands behind her back and stared at her uncle, doing her best to avoid the Hot-Doc.

Yet, as hard as she tried, she couldn't stop peeking at him, dressed casually in jeans and sneakers. It was a shame the long doctor's coat hid his backside and the fit of his t-shirt, while the baseball cap shaded his eyes.

'Are you gonna watch the footy tonight, Doc?' Uncle Frank asked.

'It's why I'm doing the rounds early.' Stewart, with the half-eaten apple in one hand, checked over the chart, flicked his pen from his pocket and approached Uncle Frank's wall of gadgets and beeping machines. 'So how long are you in town for, Kathryn?'

'How long's a piece of string,' she mumbled.

Uncle Frank chuckled, winking at her. 'Don't mind my summer-storm.'

'Storm?' Stewart peered out the window beside him.

Kat face-palmed herself, feeling the heat radiate between her fingers.

'You used to be a whirlwind,' Uncle Frank said to Kat.

'Who?' Stewart asked.

'Why, this little ray of sunshine, right here.' Frank

pointed at Kat, who wanted to hide under the bed.

Stewart chuckled as he checked over the bottles hanging above Frank's bed and made notes on his chart. 'Okay then, why a whirlwind?'

'Don't—' She warned Uncle Frank, who only grinned wider at her.

'Coz every summer like a whirlwind, Kat would come to town stirrin' up life as we know it, and now me little whirlwind's back.'

'Still a whirlwind?' Stewart asked.

'Nooo,' whined Kat.

'She's more of a mild storm front these days, and one of them women who can do twenty things at once and still gets the job done right. Although, you've been known to go the full Kat-5 cyclone if you're ticked off enough,' Uncle Frank said, laughing at her. 'She's single, you know.'

'Hey!' She glared at Uncle Frank in his bed.

'Nah, Kat's not your type, Doc.' Uncle Frank laughed even louder at her.

'I'm leaving now,' she said, and his smile faltered, 'but I'll be back tomorrow.'

'You can come by anytime, day or night. I'll just be hangin' round here, annoying the staff.'

'Sure. Do you need anything?'

'Can you check the kitchen sink for me? Oh, and kiddo, top of that list is the ol' ute, she needs a good run. Bea can't drive it these days, it's too high for her. Now, I'll need you to take it to the mechanic's first thing on Monday morning, because the Beast would love you to use her. She needs to get outside.'

Uncle Frank did too, just to get the colour back into his face. 'Sure.' After driving across the country, Kat was game enough to tackle the Beast again.

'Good. I'll expect a report on what needs to be done when you bring in the little Miss.'

'You might have to wait for that report until Monday, I've got to drop off the trailer and hire van at the train station, but we'll still visit tomorrow, I promise.'

'Lookin' forward to it, kiddo.'

Should she bring coffee? Was Uncle Frank allowed coffee? Did they even sell decent coffee in this town? Vaguely remembering the train station's Tea Room only served traditional teas, where coffee was a crime amongst those tea snobs.

'Nice to meet you, Doctor,' she said, remembering to be polite, then backed out of the room in need of fresh air. She was never returning during doctor's hours again, but while she was here… 'Um, Doctor, have you got a second?' She pointed to the door.

'Stewart. Please.' He tucked the chart back into its folder above the bed, took a bite out his apple and followed her into the corridor.

'How is Uncle Frank doing?'

'That's confidential.'

'Uncle Frank told me everything over the phone.' A phone call that had gutted her so badly, she'd dropped her entire life to drive across the country. 'My Aunt doesn't understand a lot of the technical jargon, neither did I.' She held up her hand to stop him speaking. 'You don't need to explain, I know someone in the city who helped us understand.' Over bottles of wine, and boxes of tissues shredded by tears. 'We know the treatments are no longer working and you're trying to make him as comfortable as possible.' She hoped.

'Okay then, yes, it's all we can do.' Stewart took another bite of his apple.

How rude! Kat crossed her arms over her chest and glared at the guy lacking all forms of professionalism, eating a freaking apple. 'How much time has he got? No BS.'

Stewart chewed, swallowed, took a deep breath and said, 'Six to eight weeks, if we're lucky, I'm sorry…'

Her hand slapped her heart, her knees weakened, and her stomach dropped as she leaned against the corridor wall. *Weeks. Mere weeks — to live.*

Stewart grabbed her arm. 'Are you okay?'

No. 'I'm fine,' she whispered, shrugging off his hand. 'So that's it? Uncle Frank just lies there and waits to die?'

'There's nothing more we can do, except make him comfortable. The cancer is too far advanced, but he'll have good and bad days.'

'Can he leave?'

'To go where?' Stewart asked, stepping back from her

and lifted his half-chewed apple as if to take another bite.

'On a picnic, or fishing—he loves his fishing. Maybe we'll take a nice Sunday drive to get the Beast dirty—he loves the Beast too.' She tried to remember all of Uncle Frank's favourite things, which were all things Aunty Bea. Uncle Frank was also a hard-core Blundstone boot-kicking, blue singlet wearing, tru-blu Aussie bloke from the bush who loved his beer and barbecues. *Would Uncle Frank be allowed to drink beer?* 'You have to let me take him out, please? I can't let him spend what little time he has left, staring at four walls. Not when the man has spent most of his life outdoors, building those walls.'

'I'll need to think about it,' Stewart said, taking another nibble of his stupid apple.

'Come on, he's an adult. It's not like I'm asking a parent's permission to take out a child for a sleep-depriving, sugar-fuelled sleepover!'

Stewart frowned. 'He's on a drip—'

'We'll be careful. We'll hook it up to a wheelchair, and schedule it around your med times. I'm flexible and I take direction well. *Please,* let me do this for him?' She'd beg on her knees if she had to.

'Like I said, I'll consider it.'

'Well, don't think too long, because the guy's already on death row.' She leaned in closer, narrowing her eyes at him, tempted to mush that apple into sauce right across his handsome face, and said, 'I'll ask you tomorrow, before I suggest anything to my uncle, because if I mention it to him now, he'd make me sneak him out of here faster than you could blink. Enjoy your evening, *Doctor.*' She walked away before she did something she'd forever regret.

Three

It was big. Solid. Faded. And it was *the Beast*.

The Ford F100, red ute, was a rare oddity in this world of Land Cruisers and Hilux utes, and Kat knew it well.

She'd met the Beast the same day Uncle Frank had strolled up to her boarding school, shook her hand, introduced himself, and off they went car shopping. Kat got to pick the fiery red ute, and was the first passenger on the Beast's maiden voyage home, straight out of the car yard.

Back then it was all shiny and new.

Today…

She winced at the driver's door screech that echoed inside the dark shed. Thick dust covered the torn bench seat where she'd sat while Uncle Frank drove them from job to job—sneaking in many midday billabong fishing breaks.

The poor old workhorse looked haggard and forgotten.

Uncle Frank was right, the Beast needed to get out.

'Is that an old truck, Mummy?' Kaytlyn asked, peering in from the shed's open doorways.

'This. Is. A classic.' Kat ran her hand along the scratched side panel to the rear tray and pointed to the groove in the back corner by the tail lights. 'I made that dent, backing into the letterbox when I was fourteen. It made a huge mess.' She laughed about it now, but at the time she'd been mortified.

'Is that why we don't have our own car, Mummy?'

Nice—not. 'We lived in the city, honey. We didn't need one there, and there's nothing wrong with walking.' Kat walked everywhere, but not today.

She opened the heavy passenger door that squealed like a trapped fruit bat. 'Where's the oil?' She peered into the shadows of Uncle Frank's shed where stuff lay everywhere. Uncle Frank was right, she'd have to clean this place up to find anything, and added it to her ever-growing list. If she was staying for a while, she'd need the workspace.

'How come you're allowed to use this…*car*?' Kaytlyn asked, peeking inside the cab, holding down her yellow tutu covering her new school uniform.

'It's not a car—it's a ute.' Kat spread the bedsheet across the seat so they wouldn't get dirty, both properly dressed for the first day of school. 'Uncle Frank wants me to use her. Do you think we should?'

'You bet. This is bigger than Nanny Bea's car, huh?'

'When did you start calling Aunty Bea that?'

'Last night while you were in the shower. I told Nanny Bea she looked like a storybook nana and she said to call her nanny. Mr Frank likes me calling him Poppy.' Kaytlyn explained as she climbed onto the huge bench seat that made her appear tiny in comparison.

'When did that happen?'

'While you were returning the rental car, Nanny Bea and I visited him in the hospital.'

Sneaky things. She was amazed, yet grateful, at how well Aunty Bea and Kaytlyn clicked. 'Try and find your seatbelt, huh?'

Kat gave a hard shove to shut the heavy door and walked around the Beast. She made the awkward climb in her skirt and heels to slide into the driver's seat. Once behind the large steering wheel, she patted the dusty, cracked dashboard just like Uncle Frank used to. 'You ready, old girl?'

'I am,' said Kaytlyn, straightening her tutu.

Kat giggled, turned the key in the ignition and the large Chevy rumbled to life.

Over the engine's amplified roar inside the shed, Kaytlyn shouted, '*I can see the whole world from here.*'

Even if the view was facing the workbenches, Kat knew that feeling well. The Beast was so big, she barely saw over the bonnet herself.

'Where's the air-conditioning?'

'Well, back when they made these, they had things called windows and fresh air.' Kat reached across and adjusted the mirrors as the sturdy engine made the bench seat vibrate.

She gripped the wide steering wheel as the excitement built in her chest and her smile widened. With a clunk of the gears, she reversed the Beast out of the shed and into the sunshine, looking forward to this cruise down memory lane.

Kat drove the large red ute into the only mechanics yard in town, where parked cars, trucks, tractors and other farming machinery crowded the compound. The Beast creaked, rattled and moaned as it rolled through the open chained mesh gates. Gravel crunched under its large tyres as it stopped by a row of open roller doors, leading into a massive shed.

Inside the six-bay shed, noisy air compressors competed with the blaring music, where more vehicles were raised on hoists, or with their bonnets open.

Kat turned the engine off, and it backfired like a shotgun blast. The sound echoed in the compound as a puff of black smoke rose from the exhaust. Mechanics popped their heads up from their vehicles like surgeons standing over a patient on an operating table to stare at her.

'Way to go, Beast. Nothing like making a grand entrance.' Kat cowered behind the large dashboard as the skin prickled across her face. Thankfully, today she wore makeup to hide the glow—not that she'd bother with it to deliver the Beast to the garage. She'd done this for Kaytlyn. As a single mother, she wanted to make the right impression for Kaytlyn's first day at a school that allowed her child to wear a tutu to class. *Yay for country schools.*

With a deep breath, she pushed open the door that again

screeched as if she was bending metal. She needed to find the oil gun.

Coming from the shed, a guy called out, 'Hey, isn't that Frank's old ute?'

Her heels crunched on the gravel as she straightened her dress suit, then shoved hard on the screeching driver's door to shut it. 'I don't think she wants to be here, with the backfire as her voice of protest.' Kat could relate, she didn't want to be back in this town either.

'Protest, huh?' He readjusted his baseball cap, then stopped and stared at her. '*Damn.*'

'What?' Did she have mud on her clothes? Kat dusted the back of her skirt in case she'd collected crap from the bench seat.

'Kat—Kathryn?'

'Yes.' She peered at the mechanic in his grey t-shirt that clung to his wide shoulders and the muscular, well-defined cut of his toned tanned arms. *Yum.* His jeans caressed him in all the right places, right down to his work boots. The guy should be on a wall calendar for women to admire in their office all day long. But it was his intense lapis lazuli eyes that captured her more—she knew those eyes. 'Kyle?'

'Yep, in the flesh.' He grinned at her and her knees trembled.

'Oh...' *Crap.* She stepped back into the ute and the side-mirror whacked into the back of her head. 'You really don't want to be here, do you, Beast?'

She rubbed her head, grateful for the pain disrupting her shock, as a wave of panic rushed through her. She was so close to jumping into the ute and driving away fast. Kyle was the last person she wanted to see.

'Are you okay?'

Nah—not even close to okay. 'What are you doing here?' Kat asked while rubbing her sore head.

'I was about to ask you the same question.' Kyle chuckled, removing his baseball cap, brushing fingers through his hair. 'What's it been, seven years?'

'Um...' It was Kyle, with his amazing blue eyes, thick black hair, and the same crooked smile with the dimple that only showed when he gave his sly-tequila smile.

Now a man.

Taller, broader, fitter, musclier...and—*Gulp*—too damned smouldering for her own good.

What did he say? 'Um, yeah, sure, something like that,' she mumbled, trapped under the power of those eyes that used to be her personal high. 'I've come back for my uncle.' That thought alone sobered her up, and she turned to face the Beast, pushing her feelings deep down inside.

'How's Frank doing?' Kyle asked. 'I heard he's not well.'

'They've got him...We're...he's, um, not good.' She dropped her head and stared at the gravel. It was hard to say it aloud; it just made this wretched situation more real.

'Sorry to hear that.'

'Me too.' She inhaled deeply, wincing at the scents of oil

and grease heating under the morning sun. 'So, ah, why are you here?'

'I own this place.'

'Really? Didn't your brother work here?' She searched the shadows for the shed-dwelling caveman.

'Yep, Jimmy's part of the furniture. But this is the first time I've ever seen this vehicle in my yard. Frank always parked it on the street because he didn't want to offend the old girl.'

'No one was good enough to touch her, but she's here because she needs something done,' she said with a shrug.

Kyle again chuckled, making her want to give him a goofy grin. 'Well, I'm honoured it's here. So, what's wrong with it besides the backfiring and being an old rust bucket?'

'I don't know? Uncle Frank said to bring her in, and that's what I'm doing, playing delivery driver. You're the mechanic—you work it out. And hey, just because I'm a female who's admitting to a lack of mechanical knowledge, it doesn't mean you can charge me double. All right?'

Kyle laughed so loud, it nailed a happy arrow straight through her heart that wanted to melt at his sly-tequila smile and shiny eyes.

'Wouldn't dream of it.' He lifted the bonnet, frowning as rusty metal squealed from the lack of oil. 'Still the same straight-shooting Kat, huh.' He shook his head and peered over the engine, then gave her a sideways glance with a grin. 'But you do look as amazing as ever.'

'Huh?' She bit her lip, hiding her hands behind her back, feeling butt-naked in the middle of a city train station during peak hour. *How did he do that?*

A young guy, wearing grease-stained overalls five sizes too big for him, approached and asked, 'Hey, isn't that Frank's ute, yeah?'

'Yes, JT,' replied Kyle.

'Wow, what's it doing here? Frank would never bring it inside the yard. Man, that's a Chevy V8 block. Hello, *baby.*' JT peeked inside the engine bay and his eyes widened like a kid given a free all-you-can-eat pass to a lolly shop.

'What do you want done, Kat?' Kyle asked, standing back from the engine being gushed over by JT.

'Fix her up.' She could fix things, it was fixable. It deserved to be fixed. It had to be fixed. 'I want it restored. Let's do the lot.' She could picture it all shiny and new as if back on that showroom floor. 'Can you work on the engine and exterior? I'll do the interior.'

'I'd love to work on this, boss. Can I, yeah?' JT asked.

Kyle shook his head. 'You've got enough to do, JT.'

'Yeah-nah, but this is an original. This is heaven in metal and muscle, man. This is a mechanic's masterpiece in old-fashioned machinery. You've gotta lemme do this one, yeah? *Please*?' JT tore off his cap, held it to his chest to plead with Kyle.

'I dunno, JT, it might be too big a job for you.'

'No way, me and this puppy will work together.' JT

slammed on his cap backwards, climbed onto the bullbar and leaned in to poke around the engine. He was small enough to hide inside the engine bay itself. 'When do you wanna start work on it, miss?'

Kat glanced at the parked machinery crowding the yard. 'Have you guys got time to fit this project in?'

'How soon do you want it back?' Kyle asked.

'Can you please do the engine basics first? I want to take my uncle fishing in a few days. I should have his leave pass from the doctor by then.' She was determined to get Uncle Frank out to do all the things he loved, which was Aunty Bea, fishing, and the lazy cruise in the Beast to get him there. 'I'll bring it back after our day out, then we can surprise him with the restoration.' She might not be able to fix the man, but she could fix his car.

With delicate fingertips, she stroked the dent on the front grill. 'I want to see her restored and as close as we can get to her original condition.' She'd never been sentimental over anything materialistic, surprised she wanted to have this hunk of faded rusty metal returned to its former glory. 'How long will it take?' She asked Kyle, because time was precious.

Kyle started to speak but JT butted in first. 'Yeah, you'd wanna stick with its original colour and parts, miss,' JT said as he lovingly stroked the side panel as if talking to the vehicle itself. 'A few dents here and there, but you'd want that same fire engine red, and some decent tyres too, yeah. Hey, she'd be schmick in a set of whitewall tyres, to give it that macho retro look, yeah?'

Retro she could do. 'I like it, and you,' she said to JT.

Kyle frowned from the other side of the car. 'Why?'

'JT appreciates the ute as much as I do. You called it a rust bucket.'

'*It is* a rust bucket.' Kyle pointed to the panel where rust blended with the faded red paint.

She gasped at him in mock horror. 'Where has your vision gone, Kyle? JT called it a classic. It's obvious he can see this ute for what it's worth. Hey, JT?' She leaned down to find JT on his back in the gravel under the belly of the beast. 'Would you call this mass of moving metal an old rust bucket?'

JT popped his head up from the rear of the ute. 'No way. It's a piece of automotive history. This is from an era where cars were handmade and built to last, yeah.' He walked backwards with his fingers creating a rectangle like a movie director trying to capture the perfect scene. 'The best part is there's not one damned computer chip inside this ancient beauty.' JT slapped his hand over his heart and sighed, staring starry-eyed at the Beast. 'I'm *in love.*'

'See.' Kat raised her eyebrow to Kyle while pointing at JT's obvious enthusiasm.

'Pathetic,' mumbled Kyle, shaking his head, but his sly grin made her smile more. 'Okay JT, you have the job, but finish the other car in your bay before you start on this one.'

'Thank you, boss.' JT smiled wide as he walked backwards to the shed, not taking his eyes off the red ute.

Kyle shook his head at the kid, then said to Kat, 'We'll do what we can in a basic service today. You can pick it up tomorrow. If there's something major, I'll let you know because *we'll both* go over this ute carefully.'

'You're just trying to suck-up because JT made you look bad.'

JT hollered from the open roller doors, 'Hey, what do you call it, miss? Coz a car that's been in the same family this long has gotta have a name, yeah?'

'Aww, he knows.' She pressed her hand over her heart and smiled at the kid in baggy overalls and grease.

'And you're telling me *I'm* sucking-up,' mumbled Kyle, throwing his thumb back in JT's direction.

'We call her the Beast, but my daughter calls it the Red Rocket,' she shouted to JT.

'I'll take good care of her, I promise.' JT waved, adjusted his cap, and disappeared into the shed's shadows.

'I like him. JT must be a good employee. He sold me on the service I'm now going to expect,' she said to Kyle beside her.

'JT's a major grease monkey who lives for cars—hey, did you say you have a daughter?'

Crap. 'Yep.' Through the open passenger window, with shaky hands, she retrieved her handbag from the torn bench seat. She had to go, *now*.

'Just the one?'

'I have the perfect one, so one's enough, thanks.'

'Husband?'

'No.' There were no rings on her fingers, *no sirree.* 'Can I leave the Beast here, or do you want me to move it?'

He stepped closer and his salty citrus-spiced aroma wove around her. It matched his sly-tequila smile; making him that sultry thirst quencher she wanted to guzzle during a heatwave. *Not fair.*

'Leave the keys in it and we'll move it shortly—'

'Sure—great. Thanks for fitting it in. Anyway, I've gotta get going.' *Somewhere, anywhere, just not here, with you.* Kat slung her bag over her shoulder, slid on her sunglasses, and headed for the nearest exit.

'Want me to drive you somewhere?'

A bell rang through the shed's speakers and a few seconds later JT yelled out, 'Phone call, boss.'

'I'm fine, and you're busy,' she said over her shoulder, finding it easier to breathe the further she got away from him.

'Good to see you again, Kat.'

'Sure, yeah, you too, Kyle.' *He always looked far too good.* 'I'll see you tomorrow.' She waved from the front gates, stepped onto the sidewalk, and into the sanctity of the outside world. If she wasn't doing this for Uncle Frank, she wouldn't be leaving the Beast in this yard—not in Kyle's yard.

Why did Kyle have to be here, with that same smouldering stare that always saw straight into her soul? *Damn it, why?*

*   *   *

Kyle slowly headed into the shed while watching Kat walk down the road.

'Oi, Kyle, who's the babe?' Jimmy asked, wiping his sweaty face with the shoulder of his overalls that stretched over his large biceps.

JT peeked out from under the bonnet of a small sedan. 'What babe?'

'JT, you wouldn't know what a good-looking woman was even if she came up and bit you on the arse.' Kyle shook his head at the kid. He also knew that woman's arse. He'd spent many summers following that bum on their adventurous outback hiking trails.

JT stood beside the brothers and searched the yard. 'Whose biting who on the bum, yeah?'

'Try lookin' that way, JT.' Jimmy hooked his thumb towards the front entrance.

'Yeah-nah, man I missed that,' said JT, shrugging.

Kyle wished he didn't miss it or remember. 'You were too busy drooling over the ute.' He nudged the kid's skinny shoulder, and JT grinned.

'Hey, isn't that Frank's beast?' Jimmy pointed to the faded bulky F100 parked in the centre of the yard.

'Yep.' It was still a rust bucket, but Kyle had seen Kathryn's eyes glow as if she could picture it fully restored. She still had that gift to see what others didn't, in what he now saw as junk. She was right, Kyle had lost the vision they'd once shared.

'I'm fixing it up, yeah,' said JT, gazing at the faded ute with a goofy grin.

'Choice.' Jimmy's big hand twisted JT's baseball cap like it was half a bush-lemon getting juiced.

'Oi, leave off.' JT waved at Jimmy and tidied up his hair.

'So, who owns that choice piece of rump—'

'Jimmy, *enough*,' barked out Kyle to his brute of a brother who towered over them. 'That woman'—*who happens to still have an exceptional arse on her*— 'happens to be Frank's niece. That's Kathryn.'

'No. Nope. Nooo.' Jimmy's face screwed up, and he cupped his mouth like he was going to throw up. 'Tell me I was not perving on Kat, bro? That can't be Kit-Kat?'

'Yep.' Kyle sighed, crossing his arms over his chest. 'That's Kathryn, all grown up.' Kyle had recognised her within seconds of getting close to her. The thick, untamed, lazy curls of auburn hair and the freckles she'd tried to hide under her makeup. She still had the smile and shine of mischief in her mint-green eyes that always saw more than most. Even after all these years, he'd know her anywhere—and wished he didn't.

Jimmy blew out a long breath, raising his eyebrows at Kat in the distance. 'Little Kit-Kat grew into a—'

'Don't say it, now you know who it is.' Kyle glared at his brother, surprised the same protectiveness he'd had for her, still stirred inside.

Jimmy held up his callused, grease-stained hands in surrender. 'Hey, forget I spoke. Sorry, man.'

Kyle was sorry too.

'How long has it been since Kat's been in town?' Jimmy asked.

'Seven'—*long*—'years.' Kyle slid his hands into his jeans pockets and sighed as she disappeared out of sight, again.

'Why is she here?'

'Frank's sick, and he must be sick for—' *that fine piece of arse to come strolling back into town.* 'I'd better take that phone call.' Not that he could focus on work now, with his head still spinning about Kathryn being back.

'Who's Kat?' JT asked, peering up at Jimmy.

'My baby brother's childhood sweetheart.'

'The one you called a babe, yeah?'

Jimmy screwed up his nose. 'I shouldn't have said any of that claptrap, coz Kat was like a little sister to me. I used to thump blokes for talkin' about her like that.'

'Yeah-nah, but you just said—'

'Hey, if you wanna make your twenty-first, JT, you'll forget I ever spouted out any of that garbage.'

JT laughed up at the big man. 'What's the big deal? So it's someone you used to know.'

'Kat was like family. She'd show up in town every school holiday, and Kyle and Kat were close.'

'They don't look too close if she's walked away, yeah.'

'That's what she always did…walk away.'

'Where did she go?'

'No idea. Kat left seven years ago, breaking my brother's heart, and none of us have seen her since.' Jimmy sighed, crossing his arms over his chest, shaking his head at the ground. 'But hey, that pair of summer sweethearts, man, they had sparks. Wait till I tell the missus—'

'*Oi*, I'm not paying you two to stand around yakking all day,' called out Kyle from the office doorway, glaring at his brother and his big mouth.

Kyle closed the office door and collapsed into his chair. The air conditioner hummed in the quiet room as the sounds of the air compressor and tools started outside.

He grabbed his keys from his pocket and unlocked the bottom drawer to his desk. From inside he pulled out a dated car magazine; hidden within its pages was an old photograph.

Even now his heart jumped at the vision.

He stared at his twenty-year-old self, celebrating the end of his apprenticeship, where he'd been sharing the moment with Kat.

His fingertip stroked the side of her face. In the image she was barely eighteen, with their arms wrapped around each other, leaning against his first muscle car. The midnight black Holden Monaro that used to be his pride and joy—his baby.

But it was the girl who still made his heart skip. Uncle Frank called her his little whirlwind, and she was. Just like a storm rolling in off the dry dusty floodplains to shake up his world, only to disappear.

He used to count down the months for school holidays, then at midnight, he'd stand at that town's only bus stop, waiting for her arrival. Back then he used to wish every week was summer, and when summer arrived, he wished it would never end.

The photo was from their last summer, taken the day before she left town. It was also the last time he'd seen her.

He sighed at the picture of the girl he once knew. Did he know the woman who was a mother now? A mother. She had something he could never give her, or anyone.

He slid the photo back into the pages of the magazine, dropped it into the open drawer and locked it shut.

He glanced out the window and stared at the red, rusty mound of junk parked in the middle of his yard. He frowned at it, feeling the cold iron grip crushing his ribs, fighting the resurfacing emotions he'd been able to lock away. He hated feeling anything because of *her*.

They didn't have time for a restoration, not this time of year. They could only service that piece of junk and get it out of his yard, then he wouldn't have to deal with her at all.

But he couldn't do that to Frank, who adored that hunk of metal, and that man had been there for Kyle over the years.

Unlike Frank's niece, Kathryn Jones, where her rejection still burned against his ribs. Kyle didn't need Kat to stroll back into his life, only to leave him like discarded roadside dust when she left—and she would leave again. Because everything was temporary for Kat. She always had rules and a time limit which expired when the seasons changed.

And he'd hated summer ever since, because of her.

Four

'Can you pass me the pipe wrench, honey?' Kat asked, laying on her back under the double sink in the bright yellow kitchen.

Kaytlyn, in her lime-green tutu, sat on the floor next to Kat, rummaging through the toolbox and held up various tools. 'Which one, Mummy?'

'That one.' Kat pointed to the winner of the toolbox's lucky-dip.

With wide eyes and eager smile, Kaytlyn said, 'Here you go.'

'Thanks.' Kat fitted the wrench to the slip nut on the p-trap under the sink. She then tucked the old towels and buckets beneath the pipe to catch the spillage, and pulled. 'Bugger.'

'What's wrong, Mummy?'

'Uncle Frank doesn't know his own strength.' She put her boot against the back wall behind the sink, her shoulder against the solid cupboard frame, gritted her teeth, and pulled.

'There.' It finally gave way enough for her to unscrew and drop the pipe into the bucket as it leeched out a steady stream of gunk. '*Gross.*' She hated plumbing.

'It stinks, Mummy.' Kaytlyn held her nose.

'I agree.' She grimaced, using a bent coat hanger to scrape the crap free from the pipe. 'Honey…' Kat giggled to herself at what she was about to do. 'Do you still want to help?'

'You bet.'

'Well, seeing how you've got smaller hands than me, can you get into this pipe and scrub it out in that other clean bucket of water? That'll stop it happening again.'

'You bet.' Kaytlyn eagerly started scrubbing the pipe bend.

'She's in here fixing the sink,' called out Aunty Bea, entering the kitchen. 'Look girls, we've got visitors.'

Kat and Kaytlyn leaned back to peer down the corridor from their position on the floor, as a stout brunette and a little girl followed Aunty Bea into the kitchen.

'Is that you, Wendy?' Kat asked, recognising her childhood friend, now a woman.

'In the flesh, hon. Look at you, flat on your back under a kitchen sink. You know, most people usually do their best work above the sink, not below it,' said Wendy with a wide smile.

'I see you haven't changed.' Kat laughed as she got off the floor, cleaned her hands, and hugged her old friend. 'Isn't the girl next door supposed to be all things nice?'

'Oh, hon, I'm the much-improved version, just add wine! You like?' Wendy held up the two bottles in her hand.

'I like the new improved version,' Kat replied, then leaned down to the little girl sucking her fingers beside Wendy. 'Hi, I'm Kat. What's your name?'

She pulled her fingers out and said, 'Sammy,' then shoved them back into her mouth like a lollipop.

'Hi Sammy, this is Kaytlyn.' Kat pointed to her daughter scrubbing the pipe in the bucket of water.

'You started school today. You were wearing a yellow tutu,' said Sammy between her fingers.

'Everyone heard about the yellow tutu,' said Wendy.

'Kaytlyn loves her tutus,' said Aunty Bea.

'I do.' Kaytlyn peeked through the pipe, then passed it to Kat as she jumped to her boots and ruffled the layers of her tutu. 'Do you have a tutu?'

'No, but I want one,' replied Sammy through the fingers in her mouth.

'Me too,' said Wendy with her nose in the air. 'I'd rock a tutu. Don't you girls think so?'

The two girls gawked up at Wendy then screwed their noses at each other.

'Grown-ups are so weird,' whispered Kaytlyn to Sammy.

'So are mummies,' whispered back Sammy through her fingers.

'I remember saying that about my mum,' said Wendy,

putting the wine bottles on the kitchen bench.

'Weird, I can live with.' Kat refused to be anything like her mother. 'Kaytlyn, do you want to show your tutu collection to Sammy? You might have a spare one in there for your new friend.'

'You bet. Nanny Bea's making me some new ones.' Kaytlyn turned to Sammy and said, 'If you help me weed the daisy garden on the weekend, Nanny Bea might make you one too.'

Aunty Bea widened her eyes at the little girls before her. 'Sounds like I'm going to be busy sewing tutus.'

'For real?' Sammy gazed up at Aunty Bea, with her fingers hovering over her mouth. 'Any colour?'

'Why don't you two go design some. The paint is good to go in your room, Kaytlyn,' said Kat.

'*Yes*.' Kaytlyn hugged Aunty Bea in the doorway. 'Thank you for my new room, in our new home, Nanny Bea.'

'Hey, I painted it,' said Kat. 'Where's my hug?'

Kaytlyn hugged her mother as the layers of her tutu rustled. 'Come on Sammy, let's go design tutus. We can make them life-size now we can draw on the wall.' She snatched Sammy's fingers from her mouth and led her by the hand down the hall. 'You'll want to stop that, or you'll be sucking chalk all night. I've got a rainbow tutu you can wear...' The two little girls giggled, running upstairs.

'*Oi*,' hollered Wendy, 'you can't draw on the walls and don't touch the fresh paint.'

'It's okay, Wendy, we painted Kaytlyn's bedroom walls with a kid-friendly chalkboard paint. It comes in all these cool designer colours, and they can draw all over them,' said Kat, feeling like a saleswoman in a paint store.

'It's so much fun, isn't it?' Aunty Bea said with a light laugh.

'Keeps me in touch with my inner child. We'll take over later and show our daughters how it's really done.' Kat lowered herself to the kitchen floor and put the pipe back together under the sink.

Aunty Bea placed a set of wine glasses onto the bench, asking, 'Wendy, would you and Sammy stay for tea?'

'We'd like that,' replied Wendy as she poured the wine. 'Still working on the tools, Kat?'

'Just a few things to fix around here.' That her Uncle Frank kept adding daily to her to-do list. 'I heard you got married.'

'You obviously missed the bit about me recently separating from Sammy's father, and how she's been sucking her fingers ever since. The school says it's a passing phase. I hope they're right. Did you ever meet Joseph?'

Kat again levered her boot to the wall, her shoulder to the door frame, and turned the pipe wrench until the p-pipe was securely back in place. 'No idea who anyone is; but I'm sorry your marriage didn't work out.'

'I kicked him out for his inability to keep his dick in his pants,' Wendy said with a sneer. 'The mongrel was screwing around on me.'

'Oh!' Aunty Bea blinked and blinked again, like a possum trapped under the glare of a dozen spotlights. 'So, I might, um…'

'Sink's good to go, you can put the water mains back on, Aunty.' Kat watched her elderly aunt go bright red in the face.

'So, I'll go do that, then I'll go check on the two girls upstairs,' said Aunty Bea, rushing away.

'Think I shocked your aunt?'

'No more than usual.' Kat cleaned her tools and wiped away any traces of ever working there. Just the way Uncle Frank had trained her. 'What are you doing with yourself these days?'

'I work at the supermarket in town. Besides Kaytlyn and her tutu, word's out about you being back. How long has it been?'

'A while.'

'Here for your uncle, huh?'

Kat nodded.

'Must be bad, you'll need this then.' Wendy passed Kat a cold glass of white wine.

'Cheers.' Kat clinked their glasses together and sipped, indulging in a moment of silence.

'Tell me,' said Wendy, 'did you ever finish art school to become an interior decorating designer whatever?'

'I did, as an interior designer who decorates.'

'Good for you, you always said you'd do it. Are you

going to do it here?'

Kat shrugged, unsure who'd require her services out here. 'Mostly, I flip apartments.'

'You do what?'

'I buy cheap dumps and repair them to either rent or sell.' Kat was used to moving and keeping very little. Her necessities were stored in her uncle's shed, the rest was in her storage unit interstate, ready for the next job. 'I promised Uncle Frank I'd work around here for Aunty Bea.' It's the least she could do. She just wished she could fix the man, too.

'How is Frank?'

'Six to eight weeks, that's all they've given him,' Kat blurted out, unable to stop the words crushing her chest. 'You should've seen this idiot doctor, eating a stupid apple while telling me Uncle Frank has mere weeks to live. I wanted to mush that apple into apple sauce right across his face—even if he is handsome.'

'I'm so sorry to hear about Frank.' Wendy paused, the silence was deafening. 'Are you talking about the younger Doctor Mannen?'

'I guess so, not much older than us. Why, how many Doctor Mannen's are there in this town?'

'Two. Are you talking about Doctor Stewart Mannen?'

Kat scowled. 'That's him. The one who wears a baseball cap like he's working the halls in between sports practise. Who does that?'

Wendy cackled so loudly it echoed off the kitchen

cupboards.

'What did I say that was so funny?'

'You've got to be the only woman in town to say that about our manly Doctor Mannen. All the women, including me, are ga-ga over him and there you are…' Wendy held her ribs and laughed.

'Sure, he's a Hot-Doc. So, what?'

'You like him?'

'Not now.' Kat shrugged, taking a sip of her wine.

'Oh, come on.'

'Nope, not interested.'

'You're kidding me, you just called him the Hot-Doc'

'He *was*.'

Wendy squinted her eyes at Kat. 'Seen Kyle yet?'

'Yep.' Kat turned away and checked inside the toolbox to avoid facing her friend.

'Oh well, that explains *everything*. When did you see Kyle?'

'Today. He's fixing Uncle Frank's ute.' Kat took a mouthful of her wine, tempted to empty the glass in a few gulps. 'If I'd known Kyle owned the mechanics shop, I would have gone elsewhere.' If she didn't have the overwhelming need to fix the Beast, she would never have gone into his yard. But this was her way of doing something for Uncle Frank. She turned on the tap and checked her repairs were working.

'Oh *whateverrr*, like the next nearest mechanic isn't a two-hour drive away,' said Wendy, eyeing Kat over the rim of her wineglass. 'Kyle's dating Emelia these days, she's the supermarket's new office manager. Although, she's been there forever. Emelia Templar, remember her?'

'Nope.' Kat picked up the toolbox and put it by the back door, ready for the next job, refusing to think or remember anything about Kyle.

'You must remember Emelia. She was the little blonde-haired, blue-eyed beauty they used to dress like a doll.'

'I'm not judging. Remember, I'm the mother of the tiara-less tutu-loving princess.'

'Emelia's daddy's the mayor now, he owns the supermarket which is how come she got the manager's job. Remember, Emelia used to give us both a hard time, like *every time*, we went into her store in summer. Emelia, not Em, not Emmi, not Lee but—'

'*Emelia*,' they said with a grin.

Kat remembered the girl with her pristine dresses and tidy hair in ribbons—who was everything Kat wasn't.

'Emelia used to wear that horrified look whenever we rode our push bikes over, just to stand in front of the frozen foods section whenever it got too hot and sweaty in summer,' said Wendy. 'Other kids do it now, I think we started a tradition.'

'Or we stole the idea from someone else.'

'Whatever, it worked for us, we couldn't swim in the creeks coz of the crocs, so we had to get cool somehow.'

'That's true.' The memories of her childhood summers

filtered through like a door had been opened. 'Does Emelia still sit at the counter painting her nails, reading magazines all day?'

'Oh yeah, she still does the nail thing, but in her office. She doesn't do front counter anymore, that's my job, where I have to deal with her all day as a boss who does nothing but shop online for her wedding.'

'I see nothing wrong with that. I buy and sell stuff online all the time.'

'But she's not even engaged.'

'No harm in being ready.'

'But she reads all these bridal magazines all the time, like she's obsessed with weddings. We all know Emelia's just waiting for Kyle to ask her to marry him.'

Kat's heart squeezed like it was a lump of liver inside an invisible fist where heartache seeped through the gaps. 'Good for Kyle,' she squeaked out. 'I-I'm pleased for them both.' She raised her glass, now tempted to snatch the entire bottle and drink it dry. Yet, it wasn't her right to carry on—not anymore. 'Here's to their long and happy life together.' Kyle deserved to be happy, even if he had hurt her all those years ago.

'You're kidding me!' Wendy screwed up her nose. 'This is *your* Kyle we're talking about—'

Kat averted her gaze to hide the pain squeezing her heart tighter. 'We haven't been near each other in years, Wendy.' If it wasn't for the Beast, she'd be happy to keep it that way.

'Whatever, I'm not toasting those two, I'd rather toast to

our friendship.'

'I'll toast to that one'—*and for the change of subject*. Kat raised her glass and said, 'May our daughters be as good childhood friends as we were.'

'And may our friendship last forever.' They clinked their glasses together and sipped. 'Come on, we've got a lot to catch up on.' Wendy topped up their wine glasses, then hooked her arm through Kat's and led them out the back door.

Late in the night, Wendy and Kat sat side by side with their legs dangling over the edge of the treehouse. Stars peeked through the tree's lush canopy as crickets hummed and a few lights shone, but the rest of the open countryside was asleep.

'So, you and Kyle—'

'Don't go there, Wendy.'

'But I want to.'

'I don't.'

'I do.' Wendy giggled as she topped up their wine glasses. 'Don't you think you two could've been a permanent thing?'

'Kyle lived here,' said Kat, 'I didn't. I wanted to go to design school.'

An eerie cry of the curlew carried over from the nearby paddock. Fruit bats' screeches followed their shadowy flight above the trees, as a distant howl of the dingo echoed into the night. These familiar noises filled her childhood summers, which now seemed so foreign to her.

'You could have come back,' said Wendy with a sigh.

'I had to go where the work was, to find my niche market. Besides, we were kids back then, and it never went past summer holidays, those were the rules, Kyle knew it, and I knew it.'

'Didn't you ever wonder if you'd lived here, things would've been different between you two? Like, permanent.'

Kat peered up at the skyline filled with twinkling stars, so bright and clear. As a child she'd tried to touch them. Many she'd seen fall and wished upon. 'I used to, a long time ago.' But she was never allowed to stay. She had boarding school, which was the only thing her mother ever did for her. 'But hey, it's a big wide world out there.'

'You must tell me of all your adventures, including the men. But first, I need to pee,' said Wendy, crawling to the wooden ladder. 'Remember when we used to swing off that rope like Tarzan-ettes?'

'I couldn't do it anymore.'

'Me neither, I'm flat out doing this wooden ladder.'

Kat held the top of the ladder as Wendy started her descent. Suddenly, there was a large creak, and both women stopped and stared at each other.

'Did you hear that?' Wendy asked from halfway down the ladder.

Another creak started like someone was rubbing an overblown balloon, making the hair on Kat's arms stand. 'Hear it? I can feel it.' The floor was bending beneath her feet. 'It's the treehouse. *Jump, Wendy.*'

Before they could, the rungs of the ladder gave way. The ladder's lengthy sides crossed over the other as the entire corner decking snapped off like a thin wafer biscuit. Timber, wine glasses, and women flew to the ground.

'*Argh,*' cried out Kat, landing on her back in the soft grass, where she shielded herself from the showering splinters of wood.

No curlew cried. Not even a cricket chirped. There was nothing but silence beneath the twinkling stars.

'Are you okay, Wendy?'

Wendy groaned, while remnants of the ladder shifted as she rolled over onto her back. 'I think so. It's a good thing this grass is so soft, huh?'

'This grass is wet,' Kat said, as the thick, cooling dew soaked into her shirt.

'I noticed.'

They lay there, giggling at each other, while the rest of the treehouse stayed hidden in the canopy's shadows.

'Reckon we should get up?' Wendy asked.

'Sounds like a plan.'

Kat pushed the broken ladder off her friend. 'Oww.' A sharp hot pain speared from her left wrist and up her arm.

'What's wrong?'

'My wrist. Stupid ladder.' Kat kicked the broken ladder and helped Wendy to her feet with her good hand.

'O-oh.' Wendy crouched over, holding onto her ribs. 'I've done something to my ribs. What about your wrist, is it broken?'

'It's sore, but I can still wiggle my fingers. See.'

Leaves hung from Wendy's hair as she swayed, squinting for a closer inspection. 'You're holding your wrist to do it.' They giggled at the puppet show of Kat's limp wrist. 'Ow, it hurts to laugh.' Wendy grimaced, hugging her ribs.

'You might've broken a rib. We should take you to the hospital to get you checked out.'

'Why?'

'Um, because you're hurting, and if you can feel it after all that wine we drank, can you imagine how bad it'll be, sober?'

'Didn't mean to drink that much.'

'Me neither.' Kat smiled at her friend, who'd shared an evening of endless carefree conversations as if they'd seen each other only yesterday. 'Come on, let's get this over with while the girls are asleep.' All tucked up inside Aunty Bea's house.

Wendy winced as she scooped up the wine bottle and held it up like a trophy. 'We'll take this for the journey.'

'Water might be good.'

'Whatever, I'm in pain,' mumbled Wendy taking a mouthful, then she passed the bottle to Kat.

'Hey, I'm not judging.' She took a sip and passed it back to Wendy. 'Does the shortcut through the back paddock still exist? Hopefully without the wallabies and pythons.' She squinted to the bare field behind the house, there was enough light from the quarter moon to just see ahead. It used to be full of grassy crops that would wave at her as they grew over summer. Now it was freshly cut and left in massive rolls of hay, leaving the area wide open. It was so different from the cramped, bright lights of the city.

'Do you remember the way?' Wendy asked.

'Sure.' How could she forget. It was the dirt track Kat used most when visiting Kyle's place.

Refusing to think about Kyle, she slid her good arm through Wendy's and staggered into the dark, leaving the broken treehouse scattered across the lawn like the after-effects of a cyclone.

Squinting at the bright lights, they entered the car park area of the tiny country hospital and headed for the front entrance.

'Hey, we'd better hide the bottle,' said Kat.

'Why? It's almost empty.' Wendy swayed as she upended the bottle and drank the last of the wine.

'How ladylike,' said the male voice, coming from the dark.

'Whatever, whoever you are—*Hey*, who are you calling a lady?' Wendy squinted into the shadows as Doctor Stewart Mannen stepped into the light.

'Of all the after-hour wine joints—it had to be you,'

whined Kat, dropping the wine bottle into the bin. 'Go rummaging in the dark for more apples, did we?'

'Hi Doctor Mannen, remember me? I'm Wendy from the supermarket.' She waved her fingers at him, trying to tidy her hair, only to discover the twigs and leaves nesting in the mess. Kat giggled as she helped free her friend from the foliage.

'So, what brings you two out here in the middle of the night?' Stewart asked.

'We fell out of the treehouse,' Wendy said, and again the two friends burst out laughing. 'Oww.' Wendy winced, holding onto her ribs.

'Aren't you a bit old to be in treehouses?' Stewart smirked at them.

'Never,' replied Kat. 'It was a good thing it was us, too.'

'How? You fell from a treehouse.' Stewart stood in front of the pair, trying to keep a straight face.

'We were testing it for our daughters. It wasn't our fault the ladder, that poor Wendy happened to be standing on, broke.' Kat then put her arm around Wendy, who still held onto her ribs. 'Now Wendy can't laugh without it hurting.'

'I'm trying not to laugh.' Wendy winced, sharing a snort-laugh.

'Well okay then, allow me to escort you ladies inside to check out those ribs.' Stewart led the way through the sliding doors and guided them to a six-bed examination room. Wendy and Kat sat on separate beds waiting with the nurse, Jenny, to keep them company.

Wendy leaned over to Kat and said, 'Jenny's our new head nurse. Have you settled into the place yet, Jenny?'

'I'm working on it, I've just joined the softball team.'

'Softball. Is that still running?' Kat asked.

'It is, the Dusty Dingos are a great group of girls,' said Jenny. 'However, the coach is scary. Colourful, but scary.'

'Have they won a game yet?' Kat asked.

'Not in this decade.' Wendy laughed, then winced. 'Ow—can't the doctor give me something for the pain?'

'Sorry, not while you're inebriated,' said Jenny.

'Did the doctor say it was okay for me to take my uncle out for the day?' Kat asked.

'Yes,' replied Jenny. 'We'll need to discuss times.'

'For med times, I get it.' Kat was delighted she could take him out. 'Not tonight.'

'That's a good idea.'

Coming from around the corner, Stewart waved a file in his hand. 'Okay, the x-rays are back. Wendy, you have no cracked ribs but can expect a nasty bruise. You, Kathryn, have a sprained wrist.'

'That's it?' Kat shrugged, facing Wendy. 'I told you I could wriggle my fingers fine, and that I didn't need x-rays. But I am relieved you haven't broken any ribs.' Kat then winced at Stewart and Jenny and said, 'I'm so sorry to have wasted your time.'

'Don't be, you both did the right thing,' said Stewart. 'Now, let's get you bandaged up for support.'

'Oh, pick me first,' said Wendy, raising her hand. 'Ow.'

'Okay then.' Stewart approached Wendy, with the nurse handing him the bandages.

'Doctor Mannen, how come you're still single?' Wendy asked.

'Tell Wendy to mind her own business,' said Kat, heading for the corridor.

'Aren't you curious?' Wendy asked Kat.

'Not really. But I am curious as to why he wears a baseball cap all the time. Are you going bald under there?'

'No.' Stewart paused bandaging Wendy's ribs to frown up at Kat, while Jenny sniggered.

'Hey, is it too late to sneak in and see my uncle?' Kat peered down the corridor past the nurses' station where few lights shone. Uncle Frank did say she could annoy him anytime.

Stewart frowned and gruffly said, 'It's two o'clock in the morning.'

Grouchy much. She walked to the edge of the room, ready to leave.

'Can't you cure her uncle, Doctor?' Wendy asked. 'Kat's gonna be shattered when he dies. He's like the closest thing she has to a father.'

Kat leaned her shoulder against the corner wall, wincing her eyes shut. It hurt to think of Uncle Frank leaving her life. For good. He was one of the few people she cared for, with none of the rules or restrictions she always placed upon others.

'Oh, and Kat reckons your bedside manner sucks too,' blurted out Wendy.

'Hey!' Kat frowned at Wendy from the far end of the room.

'In what way?' Jenny asked, assisting the doctor.

'Because the good Doctor was munching on some apple when he told Kat her uncle had six weeks to live. Kat wanted to mash that apple into sauce all over his face.'

'I didn't realise.' Stewart again paused while bandaging Wendy's ribs.

'Kat calls you the Hot-Doc. We all think you're cute.' Wendy giggled with Jenny, as Stewart hesitated for a third time mid-bandage wrap.

Hiding her embarrassment, Kat turned her back to the room. 'Unbelievable,' she muttered under her breath.

'Okay then, you're done. Kathryn, your turn,' called out Stewart.

'I'm good. Come on, Wendy, let's go.' Kat waved from the open doorway, ready to bolt.

Stewart grabbed her arm before she left. 'It'll take less than five minutes, then you can be on your way. At least give me a chance to try and improve my bedside manner.'

'I'm sorry I ever said that, especially when I'm not your patient.'

'You are now.' He led her to the bed and started to strap her wrist. 'How are you two getting back?'

'The same way we came,' Kat replied, watching the

doctor at work. He was so gentle, with hands so soft, yet cold. She could smell his mild musk and mint aroma, almost lost beneath the overbearing scents of disinfectants. It was like he was hidden under the layers of the long white coat, sterile chemical scents, and a baseball cap. *Who was he underneath it all?* 'How come you wear the baseball cap all the time if you're not going bald? Are you scared of light or something?'

'No, I had this bad haircut back in medical school.'

'From *school*. So, how long ago was that?'

'About...' Stewart narrowed his eyes at her. 'A while ago. Huh? You don't like it?'

'I'll admit it suits you, but you're a doctor. I understand the casual approach to put people at ease, and it may be a part of your personality, but how can we take you seriously when you walk around in t-shirts and a baseball cap, eating all the time?'

'Okay then, how should doctors look?'

'The professionals they are, that many of us respect.'

'Would you like me to take my hat off?'

'Sure.'

He pulled off his cap and ruffled his sandy blond hair.

'Wow, didn't know you had such nice eyes, they're a warm honey brown. You know...' With her good hand, she ruffled his soft strands, to get rid of the helmet-hair. 'You're so much sexier without that cap. Why hide your features?' *What am I doing!* 'Can I go now?'

'Ah, yeah.' He cleared his throat and stepped back.

'Hey, thanks for your help tonight, Doctor, and for giving Uncle Frank a leave pass.' Now she could plan that playdate with her uncle.

'I'm glad to help, I like Frank.'

She could see Stewart cared about his patients. 'Sorry for being rude about you earlier. Now that I've had a first-hand opportunity to re-evaluate your bedside manner,' she said, waving her bandaged wrist at him, 'I think you're all right.'

He chuckled. 'Thank you, but I think I'll wait for the second opinion when you're sober, shall I?'

Kat grimaced at him. 'I'm in for a killer hangover, that's for sure.'

'Take a bottle each with you for the hike back,' said Jenny, passing water bottles to Wendy, dressed and waiting.

Kat could just kick herself for breaking her own hiking rule of not being prepared with the basic essentials, such as water. She needed to be better prepared than this. Today.

'Here, take these with you.' From his coat, Stewart pulled out a small sheet of pills; their aluminium covering flashed under the bank of lights.

'What's that?' Kat asked.

'Painkillers for the morning. Take two with plenty of water, and only if you need it.' He held the packet out to Kat.

'Thank you.' Their fingers brushed. But this time his hands were warm against her skin, causing a liquid heat to slowly spread up her arm. She pulled away, swallowing the lump in her throat. 'Come on, Wendy, I think we've done enough damage tonight.' Again, Kat hooked her good arm through Wendy's and, like they did every summer, they walked arm in arm down the corridor.

'Do you still think he's a Hot-Doc?' Wendy asked.

'Much better without that stupid cap on.' She peeked over her shoulder at Stewart, who waved his cap at her, and she smiled at him. 'Huge improvement.'

'I agree, the Hot-Doc just got hotter.' They giggled their way through the front doors and disappeared into the night.

Five

In his childhood home, Kyle leaned back in his armchair, cradling a beer in his lap as he watched the TV. Nearby, Jimmy sat sprawled on the couch with his feet on the coffee table. The front door opened and Nora, Jimmy's wife, walked into the house carrying a couple of shopping bags.

'Dad. Uncle Kyle,' grunted young Thomas at the door, kicking off his boots he dumped his backpack on top.

The men grunted back.

'Hey, Uncle Kyle,' Jamie said as she skipped over in her school uniform and gave him a peck on his cheek.

Kyle grinned at his niece. 'How was school?'

'There's a new girl in school. She wears these tutus with her hiking boots, it's pretty cool. Hi, Dad.' She kissed Jimmy on the cheek.

'New kid, hey?' Jimmy said, smoothing down his daughter's ponytail.

'She seems all right,' said Jaimie, 'but her name's spelt

funny.'

'Go clean-up for dinner,' said Nora, kicking the front door shut and the two children ran ahead. 'You'll never guess who's back in town?'

'Who?' Kyle and Jimmy asked, staring at the TV.

Still wearing her blue work apron, Nora dumped her bags on the floor, kicked off her work shoes, and then patted down her short brown hair. 'Kathryn Jones is back in town. I know, you're shocked, right?'

Nora scooped up her shopping bags, headed to the kitchen, and started rattling around inside. Cupboard doors opened and closed with the occasional clink of glass from the fridge. She soon returned to the lounge room with a beer in hand. Stepped over her husband's large legs resting on the coffee table, sat on the couch, and gave Jimmy a kiss on the cheek. 'Didn't you lot hear me?'

'We heard.' Kyle took a drink of his beer and tried to concentrate on the news. 'Dinner's ready in the oven for you and the kids.' He was hungry, but couldn't eat.

'Thanks. How come you two know the news before I knew, when I didn't know?'

'Kit-Kat brought her uncle's ute in to get fixed,' said Jimmy. 'She was supposed to come in this arvo to pick it up, but rang and said she couldn't make it. She's gonna pick it up tomorrow.'

'I bet I know why. Kat wouldn't be able to drive anything today.' Nora giggled behind her can.

'Why d'ya say that, luv?' Jimmy asked.

'Because Wendy and Kat had too much wine last night and fell out of the treehouse.'

Kyle quickly sat up, his heart racing. 'Is Kathryn okay?'

'She is now,' said Nora. 'You know, that drunken duo went on a cross-country hike.'

'Kit-Kat always liked her hiking.' Jimmy then pointed his beer at his brother and said, 'You used to like it too, bro.'

Kyle hadn't hiked anywhere in years. Not since Kat left.

'But that pair went hiking in the dark, at two o'clock in the morning to the hospital. I know, right?' Nora said to the brothers who'd raised their eyebrow at her. 'Wendy's got bruises on her ribs and Kat's got a sprained wrist, and I know they're both feeling sad and sorry for themselves. Wish I'd been there though, it sounded like a fun night.'

'Well, that explains why Kat didn't get Frank's ute,' mumbled Kyle, turning his attention back to the television.

'Who told you this, luv?' Jimmy asked Nora.

'Wendy told me at work today. But get this…' Nora tapped her husband's thigh. 'Kat then got up that Doctor Mannen about him not being a professional, wearing his baseball cap while on duty.'

'Sounds like Kat.' Kyle grinned behind his beer can.

'Well, it must've worked because the doctor came into the store today without his cap on, and, you know, he looks heaps better without it.'

'Should I be worried, luv?' Jimmy asked, tucking Nora

under his arm.

'Never, honey.' She reached up and kissed his cheek again, then nestled at his side. 'Have you seen Kat yet, Kyle?'

'Yep.'

'And?'

'And what? She's just like every other customer who wants mechanical work done, only it's her uncle's ute she wants fixed up.' It'd be good if Kat got that piece of junk out of his yard. It was in his face, constantly reminding him she was back.

'Kit-Kat wants it back in its original state as a surprise for Frank,' said Jimmy. 'She pretty much wants it done straight away.'

'It's impossible,' said Kyle. 'We can't fit it in, not for a while.' Anyway, Kat would be long gone before he found the time to do it. So why rush it?

'You know, Wendy says Kat told her that Uncle Frank's pretty bad.'

'How bad, luv?' Jimmy asked, frowning down at Nora.

Kyle swivelled around to face his sister-in-law. 'It mustn't be good for Kat to come all this way.'

Nora sighed, staring at her hands in her lap. She cleared her throat and said in a quieter tone, 'There's nothing more they can do for him. They reckon he's only got six weeks to live.'

'No way!' Kyle mirrored his brother's frown. *How come no one told them?*

'Kat's pretty cut up about it. Did you know, she's pretty much demanded that the doctor let her take Frank on day trips? She wants him to teach her daughter to fish. Kaytlyn's a cute little thing in her tutus and boots. She's starting a whole new school trend, coz Wendy's little girl has started wearing a tutu to school too. And you know what? Sammy wasn't sucking her fingers, either.'

'You've seen Kat's kid, luv?' Jimmy asked.

'Kaytlyn's her name and she looks like Kat at that age.'

'Where's the father?' Jimmy arched an eyebrow at Kyle.

Kyle took a swig of his beer; grateful his brother asked the questions he couldn't.

Nora shrugged. 'No idea. Wendy said Kat kept changing the subject and little Kaytlyn said she's never met her father. You know, it must've been hard doing it on her own all these years. I know I wouldn't have been able to do it without you pair helping.'

'You had twins, luv, most women get one at a time.'

'Are you sure you're all right, Kyle?' Nora asked.

'I'm fine.' When would everyone stop asking him that?

'I still can't believe little Kit-Kat's a mother,' said Jimmy. 'How is she surviving as a single mum?'

Kyle still couldn't picture Kat as a mother either. She'd be a good mum, from what he'd seen, when she used to help him babysit his niece and nephew.

'Well, she is, and she finished her interior decorating thing,' said Nora.

'Designer,' mumbled Kyle.

'Isn't that the same thing?'

'A designer knows the structural details of the property and gets into the specifics of uses in their designs to decorate. Big difference.' Kat had told him many times, it's what she had her heart set on, that and a family. Things he'd never be able to give her.

'Well, she did it,' said Nora. 'Got qualified and got her own business.'

'Kat always said she'd do it.' Kyle was proud of her.

Nora sat back and crinkled her nose at the room. 'You know, we should do that here. Spruce up the place.'

'There's nothing wrong with it,' said Jimmy with a frown, as Kyle chuckled behind his beer.

'Well, I want some chalk paint for the kids' rooms,' said Nora.

'What? Why?' Jimmy screwed his nose up. 'And what the heck is chalk paint?'

'Wendy said Kat painted her daughter's bedroom in chalk paint. I want that here too.'

'They must be stickin' around if they're painting her kid's room, eh, Kyle?' Jimmy nodded to his younger brother.

'We're talking Kathryn Jones, who never stays longer than a season. She'll do the place up and move on.' It was typical Kat, playing her part as the tropical storm doing a dust stirring drive-by.

'*Uncle Kyle,* can you help me with my homework?' Called out young Jamie from the corridor.

'Coming.' Grateful to get away from this conversation, he went to the kitchen to grab a beer on the way, as their voices followed him.

'When did Kyle see Kat?' Nora asked Jimmy.

'Monday morning. She was wearing this swanky business suit.'

'How has he been with you?'

'Sulking,' said Jimmy, 'keeping himself busy and working hard as normal.'

'Has Kyle been working on Frank's ute?'

'Nope. JT's been workin' on it and loving it too. JT had this long phone conversation with Kit-Kat all about it.'

'Did she talk to Kyle?'

'Why? Kat would know Kyle's seeing Emelia by now, especially after a night on the grog with Wendy.'

Nora asked, 'Do you know if he's still going to ask Emelia to marry him?'

Jimmy shrugged and sipped his beer.

'I hope not, couldn't stand that woman as my sister-in-law, but I know he's got the ring.'

'How?' Jimmy sat up with a frown.

'Wendy heard it from Mrs Fitzgibbons, who spotted Kyle at the jewellers in the next town,' said Nora.

'Bugger.' Jimmy mumbled and dropped his head.

'So, there is a ring?'

In the hallway, Kyle face-palmed himself. He was meant to help the kids, but he couldn't stop listening to Jimmy and

Nora's voices carrying down the corridor. He should have walked away, but he had to know if his big brother could keep his secret?

'Yeah, there's a ring,' said Jimmy, slurping on his beer.

Big-mouth, bro. Kyle frowned at the back of his brother's boofhead.

'I knew it! Have you seen it?' Nora asked her husband, who shrugged his beefy shoulders. 'Well, if I know, Emelia must know. You should've seen her today, we got this new batch of bridal magazines and she practically clawed the boxes apart just to read one. Hey, do you think Kyle's ever gotten over Kat?'

'Honestly…No.'

'I agree. Did you ever find out what happened between them for Kat to disappear like she did?'

'Nope.'

'I wonder if Kat knew Kyle was driving—'

'The night it went belly-up for Kyle,' said Jimmy with a deep sigh.

'You know, I was so sure Kat would've shown up.'

'We all assumed so, but she never did.'

Kyle hung his head, clenching his fists at his sides, feeling the pain burn in his chest at the memory. The thought of Kat back in town stirred his emotions like a rolling dust storm churning his stomach. It fought against the cold, steel crush around his ribs, where the scars were like ice slashing deep beneath his skin. He cracked open his beer can and took a long deep drink. He *wanted* to forget his past, he *needed* to forget how to feel, and sauntered away, but their voices still followed him.

'You know, I've always wondered, now that Kyle's thinking of marrying Emelia—'

'Not our business, luv.'

'Pft, haven't you ever wondered what Kyle and Kat would be like now as adults because back then, those two were inseparable.'

'Kyle was happy back then, he wasn't all bloody work and no play. Things change.'

'I know this about my brother-in-law, Kat would've made Kyle happier than Emelia ever will.'

Kyle used to think the same thing too, except Kat had deserted him when he'd needed her the most.

Six

Having survived yesterday's hangover, Kat was in damage control. The last time she'd walked this hospital corridor she was covered in dirt, leaves, wet grass, and muddy boots. In the city, no one would've given her a second glance, but here, in this town, she'd bet a thousand dollars everyone knew about the other night.

Which is not the impression Kat wanted to create as an adult.

She approached the nurses station in the small country hospital and cringed. It was Jenny, the new nurse.

'Hi…um, Jenny.' Maybe they'd forgotten all about her escapade.

'Oh, hello there. I see you've recovered from your hangover.'

Great. 'About that, I want to apologise for wasting your time.' She pulled a gift from her daypack, which had replaced her handbag after she'd broken her own rules of hiking without the essentials—in the dark.

'For what?' Jenny tightened her lips as if to stop herself from laughing.

'For bothering you over a sprain and—'

'For being a human being who was catching up with a long-time friend? Been there, but I've never fallen out of a treehouse.'

'That wasn't our fault, the wood was rotten.'

'Like you said, it was better you than your daughters.'

Kat agreed, even if Kaytlyn wasn't talking to her over the damage done. 'Here, this is for you.' She handed over a box of chocolates. 'I didn't say anything rude to you, did I?'

'Me, no.' Jenny's laugh echoed down the corridor. 'Mind you, the poor doctor has never been the same.'

Kat wanted to cower behind the desk, swearing to herself she'd never visit during doctors' hours again. 'Is Doctor Mannen on shift?'

'No.'

'Good. Can you give him this for me? You can do it anonymously.' Kat put the gift bag on the counter. 'Tell him I'm sorry for my behaviour, or better yet, tell him nothing.'

Jenny laughed and peeked inside. 'Cute bag. Are those craft ladies having a stall sale I missed?'

'Who?'

'The bag. Where did you get it?'

'I made it,' Kat replied with a shrug. 'It's part of my gift line for housewarmings.'

'I'd heard you do interior decorating,' Jenny said, sniffing at the bag. 'Yum, what is that scent?'

'From my candles, and I'm an interior designer who decorates.'

'Oh, you're just what our nurses need. Do you have a card?'

'Why?'

'The Nurses Union is gathering approvals for the outback nurses dormitory upgrades, but to be eligible there's all this paperwork.'

'You need someone to put in a proposal?'

'Yes, please.'

'Sure, I can do that.' She dug around in her daypack and pulled out one of her cards. 'Email me what you want, the address, and we'll make a time.'

'What about the bag and candles?'

'They're a part of my housewarming range. I used to give it as a gift for clients, but now those clients share with their clients. You can find my online shop on the website.'

'Are you one of those mumpreneurs?'

'Have to be.' Kat wanted the flexibility to be with her daughter, and she had no husbandly support in bringing up a child.

'I'll check it out,' said Jenny. 'Living out here, I'm getting used to online shopping. I'll let the other nurses know to tidy-up for the inspection.'

'They don't need to clean up for me. Not when you've

seen me at my worst.'

'Believe me, I've seen plenty of sorrier patients in my time. You and Wendy were fun, and you bring gifts.' Jenny lifted the gift bag and again sniffed inside. 'You should see the craft store about running a class on candle making, I'd love to do it. You can never have enough candles, especially out here with the blackouts through all those summer storms. I learned my lesson last summer. Talking about times, I'll write down the best times for you to check your uncle out. Do you have a time preference for a tour of the Nurses' rooms?'

'Anytime I can get for Uncle Frank, day or night, you name it; and school hours for business site visits.' It's how she trained her clients, but that didn't mean she stopped working from home long past business hours. 'Well, enjoy the chocolates and again, I apologise.' Kat slunk toward her uncle's room, keen to plan his first day trip of freedom together. She'd missed out yesterday, and no doubt Uncle Frank would want a full report on the treehouse incident too.

A few hours later Kat left her uncle to rest for the afternoon. She shut his door behind her, leaning against it as her shoulders sagged with her sigh. The emotional effort it took to visit the man was enormous.

It also hurt more having to leave him behind in that room, when what she really wanted to do was steal him away to find some miracle cure.

Uncle Frank was tired today, yet, he still smiled with that spark in his eyes. He told his many stories while they played cards together, in his room that was slowly being transformed by Kaytlyn's daily drawings. Was there anything else she could get him to make him more comfortable?

She'd seen his excitement at tomorrow's adventure, giving her a list of gear for their fishing trip. On top of that list was to fetch the Beast and load it up for their big day out.

She pushed off the wall and headed down the corridor, focusing only on tomorrow.

'Kathryn?'

She turned to find Stewart approaching her without his baseball cap on.

'I got your bottle of wine,' said Stewart, 'you shouldn't have, but thank you.'

'Look at you, no hat, and in a collared shirt. The women of this town should be thanking me.'

He chuckled, shaking his head. 'I've had many compliments.'

I bet. The guy was a good-looking doctor, he'd have to receive compliments all the time. So why was a guy like Stewart working in a town like this? 'Look, Doctor—'

'Stewart, please. We can be friends, now?'

'Sure, if you're game enough.'

'I think I can handle your brutal honesty.'

'I'm sorry for being a nuisance the other night.' Although she wasn't sorry for what she'd said about the baseball cap, he looked damn fine without it.

'How's the wrist?'

'There,' she said with a shrug. 'Aunty Bea made me wear the bandage, but I'm fine.'

'Okay then, let me take a look at it.'

'But…'

'Come on, you're here now, I am still the doctor, or should I expect another lecture?'

'I'll try not to.' They headed for the examination room she'd been in the other night.

'How does it feel?' Stewart asked, removing the bandage and examined her sore wrist.

'It's annoying.' *And frustrating*, stopping her from doing the simplest of tasks.

'Okay, the swelling has gone down, but the bruising isn't pretty.' His fingers were soft and gentle, yet cold on her wrist. She winced at her own hands in dire need of moisturiser and a manicure. It was embarrassing.

Stewart slid an elastic wrist bandage over her hand. 'Please wear this for the rest of the week, at least.'

'Sure, thanks.' The low heat from his touch was again injecting a slow feed of liquid warmth through her veins.

'How did you find your uncle today?'

'Tired. I'm taking him fishing tomorrow, he's looking forward to it.'

'Just you two?'

'Aunty Bea and my daughter are coming too; we're

having a picnic and going between his meds like I promised.' This short daytrip was nothing like the three-day outback treks to Uncle Frank's many secret fishing spots. The journeys themselves were part of the adventure in the search for the prize jewel, the mighty fighting barramundi.

'Here, take my card,' said Stewart, 'it has all my numbers in case you have any problems or concerns.'

She flipped his business card over; it was so plain compared to her own. Then again, health professionals didn't need to sell themselves, when they were already in high demand. Kat raised her eyebrows at the five numbers on the card and one written on the back.

'Yeah, I know, too many numbers. It'd be easier if we had consistent mobile range out here, especially when there are only two doctors in the region.'

Again, raising the question, why was he here?

'You're doing a good thing, working at this bush hospital,' said Kat, 'it means a lot to the locals. Not that I'm a local, I'm just a visitor.' She jumped off the bed and headed for freedom. 'I'm sorry if I was harsh on you. Well, enjoy the wine, and I'll see you in the halls sometime.' Not if she could help it, although she wouldn't mind the eye-candy crush in the corridor.

'Hey, Kathryn,' Stewart called out as he jogged to catch up to her at the doorway.

'What's wrong?'

'Nothing. I was wondering if you'd like to have coffee

with me sometime?'

'Where do we get decent coffee in this town?'

'My place.'

She arched her eyebrow at him. 'Oh, really?' Was that a normal pickup line for this guy? *What a player.*

'I happen to own a decent coffee machine, and during med school, I lived on the stuff. If they'd taken any blood from me back then, it would've been pure caffeine.'

She laughed with him as the butterflies stirred in her lower tummy. *Not good.* 'Sounds good.' *Ugh*, she'd meant to say no, but then she remembered something. 'Uncle Frank was telling me you have a problem with your back door?'

'I do.'

'How about you make the coffee and I'll have a go at fixing the door. I'm not promising you anything, but I'll try.' If she fixed the good doctor's door that'd make her uncle happy. And, the guy was also giving her the green light to set Uncle Frank free for a few hours. She'd do it for a decent coffee.

'Okay then, when?'

'School hours.' She should have it written on a placard above her head.

'How about tomorrow morning?'

'Coffee in the morning, how unusual,' she said, trying not to smile. 'Consider that a yes.'

'Okay, I'll see you then.'

'Thanks for this.' With a wave of her bandaged arm, she headed into the sunshine, surprised she'd agreed to a coffee date. It'd been ages since she'd agreed to any date. Would she show up, or bail like normal?

It was easier not to get attached, or ever suffer that feeling of rejection again. So why did she agree to do so now?

Seven

Kat walked down the main street of town to pick up the ute. She was dreading it. Not the Beast part, the Kyle part; a memory she refused to dwell on.

Also, if she was staying in town for a bit, she needed cash flow. It'd be a bonus if the Nurses Quarters came through, but dealing with government departments was a long and painstakingly slow process.

A whistling toot pierced the silence, and she searched for the foreign sound. She soon recognised it was the train. Was it coming or going? Would Kaytlyn be interested to see the train and watch the cattle load or to peek at the passengers?

Kat then realised she'd stopped in front of the one store she'd visited regularly with Aunty Bea. It was the town's craft store that sat alongside the post office.

She cocked her head at the same window display she'd always remembered. It hadn't changed at all. *How is that possible?*

Fond memories of this store brushed over her, staring at

a place that was jam-packed full of materials. Some women shopped for clothes. Kids shopped in toy stores. Kat shopped for furniture fabrics, and she had reams of the stuff stored away in boxes in her storage unit. One day she'd have her dream office studio, complete with display cupboards for her materials and paints. Along with a special rack for her trinket collection of doorknobs, handles, and specialty brackets. She had boxes of the stuff she hadn't opened in years.

Nope, she didn't need to go inside.

Nada.

No.

But Jenny did mention a candle making class, *and if* Kat did get the nurses' refurbishment contract, she'd want to buy locally…

Unable to help herself, Kat pushed on the glass door and the all too familiar bell jingled overhead as the smell of materials seduced her senses. She took a deep breath and was ready to indulge in one of her favourite pastimes, craft shopping.

Two hours later she emerged from the store with two reams of material wrapped in brown paper, and a job. Mrs Sternston remembered Kat and offered her a job dressing her window display once a month. It wasn't like the ultra-fashionable inner-city boutiques she was used to, nor was it like her first job working on downtown department store displays. But it was a job, and she wasn't going to complain.

They'd also shared a conversation about future craft

classes, and not just in candle making. Kat was an upcycling repurposing designer who not only flipped apartments, she'd taught many classes about her unique crafting style in the city. Would there be enough of a market for her, here in this tiny town?

Continuing her downtown tour of Elsie Creek, she entered the hardware store that doubled as a feedstore on the side. She needed some wax for the doctor's sticky door problem.

By the open doorway, Kat passed the large round table with chairs tucked underneath. A pack of playing cards and an empty ashtray rested in the middle with the scent of stale cigar smoke in the air. She recognised the scent like she recognised the layout of the store's shelves which had never changed.

She approached the counter where the owners, the brothers Michael and Paul Flynn waited on the other side. They could've passed as twins, but their dress styles couldn't be more different.

Michael's hair was perfectly parted and combed to the side with his collared shirt, starched and buttoned all the way to the top. The guy could pull off a fabulous bow tie if he wanted to.

So unlike his brother Paul, who had that I-just-got-out-of-bed and this-is-as-good-as-it-gets look. Paul's messy hair had entangled his reading glasses at a sideways angle. His t-shirt was so wrinkled it must have been pulled from the bottom of the washing pile. He wore an odd pair of football socks in his work boots—made even more unreal, when they sold work boots and matching pairs of socks on the rack directly behind him.

'Lookie who we have here,' said Michael, pushing his glasses higher along his nose.

'Wonderin' when we'd see you in here,' said Paul, tucking his thumbs into his thick leather apron. 'Come to get some wood for the treehouse you fell out of?' They both laughed at her.

The heat flared in her cheeks as she waved her bandaged arm. 'I live to tell the tale.'

'I remember when you and your uncle built that treehouse. She would've been five,' Paul said to his brother.

Michael nodded. 'Reckon so, it's done well, considering it's been up there that long. You'll wanna replace the floor for your little one and her tutus. It'll need to be solid for her dancing.'

'She doesn't like ballet, remember,' said Paul, nudging his brother.

Everyone knows everything. 'Good idea, but I'll just take this wax for today.'

'Trade discount for you,' said Michael.

She arched her eyebrow at them in surprise.

'Frank's one of our regular customers, he has a chair at the table.' Michael pointed to the vacant round table by the front window.

'Wow.' She remembered them, the *retired knights of the*

round card table, who bitched about the weather and government taxes while smoking cigars and playing cards. When younger, after watching the movie *Goodfellas*, she thought they were the outback's version of the mafia. 'Do they still smoke inside? Aren't there laws or something?'

'Technically, this is a shed. Not like we're air-conditioned, and we don't serve food—not to humans, anyway.' Paul tossed his thumb back to the feedstore side of the shed that contained stacked bales of feeding hay, pallets of 50kg bags of chook pellets, horse food, even varieties of dog food, plus all the washes, worming medicines, halters and bridles. It was a big, bulk pet shop, that farmers could drive-thru like it was a fast food joint for animals, all served with a layer of outback dust.

'Why? Are you gonna dob on us for lettin' a bunch of old fellas enjoy their cigars?' Michael frowned at her over his glasses.

'Er, no.' She wouldn't dare, it was none of her business.

'Have you voted for your choice of movies in the marathon yet?'

'Er, no.' She leaned back from Michael, who used to be a very daunting figure when she was a child. They both were.

But she was a grown-up now. A mother. An entrepreneur. She stood taller. 'Sorry, gentlemen, I've been a little busy with my own family commitments.'

Paul patted his brother on the shoulder, and Michael nodded his apology and said, 'Yeah, we're sorry to hear

Frank's still crook.'

'Crook?' *The man's dying!*

'How is Frank doing?' Paul asked.

'Not good.' How is it that in a town where everyone knows everything, so few were aware of her uncle's condition? How come she won the job of being the bearer of bad news?

'We've been meaning to visit him and all,' said Michael, giving a stiff shrug to Paul.

'But with work and stuff and, well…' Paul finished his brother's sentence while shrinking his neck into his shoulders. 'We kinda hate the hospital.'

'I don't like it much myself.' Kat liked it less each and every day.

'If you, Bea, or Frank ever need a hand or anything, let us know, okay,' said Paul.

'Yeah, anything.' Michael mirrored his brother's nod.

'Thank you, gentlemen.'

Clip-clop. Clip-clop. The noise came from outside the open double doors that led to the street, where a wide shadow stretched across the pavement.

'*Now, you get,*' called out Michael, grabbing a straw broom and raising it above his head.

Kat flinched. 'What's wrong, I'm only here—'

'Not, you. *That.*' Michael pointed his straw broom at the door, while Paul chuckled from behind the counter.

Kat's eyes widened, almost dropping her daypack as she stepped back. In the doorway stood a big, black, shiny nosed water buffalo, wearing bright fluorescent pink ribbons on its black horns. On its sides in bright pink chalk were the words, *'It's a Kimble Girl!'*

'Oh, look, the Kimble's had a baby girl. They'd be stoked, they've got a stack of boys already,' said Paul. 'Reckon they'll have enough for their own softball team soon.'

'W-w-why is there a water buffalo at the door?' Kat stammered, amazed how calm Paul was. 'Why isn't it using the other door where all the pet food is kept?'

'Cecil doesn't eat pet food, although he's gettin' a bit chunky. Those kids must be overfeeding him at the school.' Paul tilted his head as if inspecting the buffalo's torso. 'Hey Michael, do you think Cecil's getting fat?'

'School? What, they let that beast into the school?' She was going to grill Kaytlyn later about this. 'Why is it here, and can you fat-shame a water buffalo?'

'Cecil wants our flowers. Stupid thing, *get.*' Michael swished the straw broom at the buffalo, who gave a choked moo, huffed, and with a flick of the pink ribbons wrapped along his tail, he waddled away.

'Cecil's gotta thing for flowers.' Paul pointed to the rack of potted flowers for sale. 'He adores our dry season Petunias. Reckon you can let Bea know we're getting new ones in at the end of the week. She wanted some to spruce up her daisies.'

'Er, yeah, sure.' Kat was still shaking her head at the ribbon-wearing water buffalo in its no-rush amble down the road.

'Seeing as how you're here...' Paul shrugged to his brother, who nodded at him as if talking telepathically. 'We're wondering about this chalk paint you've brought to town.'

'Chalk paint?' *How did that get out of the house?*

'We've had six women come in since we opened this morning, all wanting to get some of this chalk paint for their kids' rooms,' Michael said, putting his broom back behind the counter.

'In designer colours,' said Paul.

'Oh, the kid-friendly chalkboard paint.'

'Where'd you get it?' Michael asked.

Kat grinned at them and channelled her inner *Goodfella* groupie. 'Listen, fellas, I'll do you a deal.'

Paul and Michael shared a wary arched eyebrow at each other.

'We can go to the manufacturer, direct,' said Michael.

'You can try, but you'll find I've got the supplier's ticket for this niche market.' More like a direct dial to the fairly-ugly-godfather himself. 'I can supply it to you guys exclusively. That way I'm not bothered by school mums who'll need to come here for the brushes and other equipment, anyway. Trust me on this, gentlemen, being a mother myself, once word gets out in this town, they'll show up. There's also the mothers from neighbouring towns to consider too—'

'How much?' Paul asked.

'Got an email address?' Would the Flynn brothers even bother with emails?

'Here's our business card,' said Michael.

'Great, I'll send prices and an order sheet you can show to your customers.' She glanced at their business card, *how boring*. Just like Doctor Mannen's, and Mrs Sternston's. What this town needed was a graphic designer who knew about branding. But then this town didn't like change, stuck in some time warp where it all stayed the same. How were they going to handle her window displays and eclectic tastes?

'How long will it take?' Paul asked.

'I'll aim to have the first delivery here in less than a week.' It should be a week, by train, she hoped.

'Deal,' said Michael and Paul, both putting their hands out for her to shake.

'Thank you, gentlemen.' She grinned as she shook their hands one at a time. This day was working out better than expected. If only she didn't have to collect the Beast, but she couldn't put it off any longer.

Eight

Kyle sat in his office trying to do his end of day paperwork, with no sign of Kat. Was her wrist too sore to drive today?

He'd been waiting on her phone call, hoping to beat JT or Jimmy to it, while at the same time, trying to avoid all calls from Emelia, who was constantly leaving messages.

Ever since word spread about Kat being back in town, he'd avoided Emelia. He was at a loss as to what to do.

Kyle was about to propose marriage to one woman, who was just there. When the only woman he'd ever loved—and lost long ago—suddenly reappears into his life. The one woman who'd never committed to him, who lived in another city, in another state, while he stayed in this tiny Territorian outback town.

His current girlfriend of almost three years, Emelia, did all the chasing, because he'd done all the chasing with Kat and it got him nowhere.

Most of his mates were settling down, where weddings

were becoming a common event, and he didn't want to be the bachelor who lived with his married brother all his life. Under that combined pressure, somehow, he found himself standing in a jewellery store buying a ring. He tried to get excited while searching for something suitable. Instead, he let the saleswoman choose whatever she wanted, within his budget.

That ring was still in its original bag, unopened, rolling around under the back seat of his ute because he hadn't found the words, or emotion, to ask Emelia.

Now everyone knew he had that damned ring.

Instead of thinking about Emelia and his future with her as his wife, he couldn't stop listening to all the talk about his long-lost love.

Who should've stayed lost.

Last night, he'd lost sleep because of her, tossing and turning in bed, so he'd gone down to the basement to truly rip the band-aid off his past. Hidden amongst the junk was an old box he'd kept of their memories, where he re-read Kat's letters from boarding school. He never had the heart to burn them — he'd tried, but never could.

He'd flicked through the old photos that held his favourite memories of their time together, every summer holiday.

She was summer herself. Barefoot and free with her sun-drenched skin and easy smile, shedding the world's weight of winter. She was spontaneous and unplanned, just the way summer should be.

Whenever Kat entered his world, it was like she opened the curtains on life, smiling at the sun, eager to make an adventure of their morning hikes, exploring countless trails. It was a part of their summertime ritual, as well as sharing long lazy afternoon naps, or to stargaze until sunrise. They used to have water fights in front yards, pillow fights at campsites where they danced around the campfire like no one cared. It was a time when the scents of sunscreen, spareribs and barbecues, blended with the smell of oncoming rain. Cricket was played on televisions everywhere, as well as on the street with other kids, or it was a softball bashed in the park. It was a time of melting ice creams, lemonade and milkshakes, when mangos and watermelon smiles had juices dripping from their chins. Every summer brought a new chapter to their story, never sharing any summers of regrets, but then summer always ended…

Tossing the photos aside, at the bottom of the box, Kyle found the first diamond engagement ring he'd ever bought.

He'd worked months of overtime to pay for it, and had it specially made, exactly the way she'd love it. It was a ring created, selected, and purchased purely from the heart.

Kyle was a man who had the words but sucked at speaking them. He'd had a speech prepared, practised, and memorised, and even after all these years, he could still recite it word for word.

But he never got to propose.

He never even got close.

Instead, he locked them away years ago, along with any emotions he'd ever had, just so he never had to think or feel them again.

Until now.

Somehow, she'd unlocked the box in his heart and head, and the memories had come flooding back. He'd unlocked the box hidden in the basement with a heavy heart, and sat there until three this morning.

Then he went to work like he did every day.

It's all he did these days, work. It was his way of not allowing the self-pity to build in his bones, so he worked until he was exhausted, slept, then worked again.

But not today.

Today he didn't go to work on the other cars in his yard, he worked on hers.

The Beast.

The ugly, dented, rusty piece of junk that stood in his shed. He'd frowned at it, scowled at it, prowled past it like he wanted to bash it to get back at her.

Only he couldn't.

The large red ute belonged to her uncle, Frank, and he knew how much it meant to the man. Frank had been there for Kyle many times, and he owed him.

Kyle also recognised the huge sentimental value it held for Kat—which was rare for her. She didn't hold onto anything, especially a vehicle.

Kyle never wanted to get emotionally attached to

another vehicle again. They were just mechanical pieces of steel and plastic that rolled in and out of his workshop. He didn't want to feel any kinship to a machine that could be catapulted into a tree and crumpled up like tinfoil on the side of the highway. He didn't want to call some piece of scrap metal a pet name.

Yet, he knew the Beast. He knew the owner. He knew her, and he'd seen the look in Kat's eyes as she spoke about the ute.

It also held a lot of memories for Kyle as well.

Kat had learned to drive in that ute under Frank's tuition, and Kyle had helped her too. He'd sat in the passenger seat while Kat practised driving towards their hiking adventures. They'd laid in the back and stared at the stars, camping together. They'd sat on the roof many times to watch the summer lightning storms cross the horizon. Or they'd huddled on the bonnet sharing a tarp, ducking the summer rain at the local football games.

They'd also made out many times across that bench seat too.

So, he stared at it some more and then he started…

All morning Kyle worked on the Beast, obsessed with it as the memories came flooding back. He remembered where the dents came from, the back one was when Kat smashed the letterbox. How she'd rushed over to his place in a panic, upset that Frank would belt her for it, but didn't, because Frank was never like that.

He smiled at the deep scratches on the passenger door done when she'd driven too close to the billabong's surrounding scrublands. It was the day they'd attempted to drive to the waterfall without having to hike so far to go swimming in a place free from crocodiles.

Their first kiss was in the front seat of that ute and they'd lost their virginity together in the back tray. Kyle soon came to realise the massive red hunk of metal also held a high sentimental value for him too.

Yet, he'd swore he'd never hold sentimental value to another car again.

Not like his black Monaro. It had been his dream machine, his pride and joy, and his baby. He'd learned how to panel beat and spray paint on that black car, all his creative energy went into that car.

Kat used to bring it out of him too, like she had some unknown fiery magical storm dust she'd sprinkle over him in their sleep, or whenever he was near her. He used to believe she was his muse.

Back then he'd thought he'd love the same woman for the rest of his life, too.

But that all died a long time ago.

Kyle ordered the paint for the ute and tried to work out when to fit in the spray painting before Frank passed away. How long would it be before Kat went away too? Just like she'd always done.

It was five o'clock and he logged off his PC for the day,

again Kat was a no-show. He should be used to her not being around. Again.

There was a knock on the door. It swung open and there stood Kathryn. The breeze blew in behind her, shifting her lazy curls of messy auburn hair, as wisps floated across her few freckles. Her mint-green eyes shone with that same smile he'd always remembered, and his heart just stopped.

'Hey, I thought you could do with one of these,' she said, holding up a six-pack of beer.

'Didn't think you were going to show.'

'I had a busy afternoon.' She sat in the spare chair and glanced around the room. 'This is such a big, blokey broom closet.'

He chuckled. 'I'm a mechanic, not an interior designer who decorates.' Few realised the difference, but it was also a pet hate of hers.

She smiled—and the heat shot through his heart, electrifying his veins.

'How's the wrist?' He pointed to her bandaged hand.

'Annoying.' She shared a short laugh as she attempted to open her beer can.

'Here, let me do that. Don't want you spilling beer over my filing system.' He grabbed the can and cracked it open.

'Your desk reminds me of Uncle Frank's mobile office, it used to be the dashboard of the Beast…' Her smile faltered, as did the shine in her eyes. 'Thanks.' She took the can from him and sipped with a shaky hand. 'You need something over that couch, there's too much white space. Cool couch though.'

Kyle rolled his eyes, she couldn't help herself. He didn't do art, not anymore. 'I like that couch.' He'd slept on it many times.

'Is that for when you escape your brother's place, huh?' She grinned at him as if she'd read his mind, and he shrugged. 'The gossip is, you're about to get engaged?'

Damn. 'Just gossip.' Although, he was meant to be popping the question to Emelia this Friday night. 'Talking about gossip…word around town is, you're a single mum who falls out of treehouses in the middle of the night, only to then give our town doctor a hard time.'

'That's true,' she said, raising her bandaged wrist. 'Anyway, I'm here to settle the bill.' She pulled her credit card from her daypack and placed it on the corner of the desk as if to avoid all contact with him.

It might be safer that way.

The office door burst open to JT grinning in the open doorway in his grease-covered baggy overalls. 'You beaut, you're here. I've been waiting for you.'

'Hiya JT, or do they call you Dirty Harry? Here, take this.' Kat handed him a beer.

'Cheers.' JT cracked it open and took a good slug from the can.

'How's the Beast?'

'Did you tell her, Boss?' said JT with wide eyes, wiping his mouth on his sleeve.

Kyle frowned at the interruption in the doorway. 'I was about to—'

'Come on then, lemme show you.' JT grabbed Kat's hand and dragged her out like a kid needing to show off his latest school project to his mother.

'Bring the beer with you, Kyle,' called out Kat, laughing at JT. 'Careful, watch my wrist.'

'Bloody JT,' Kyle mumbled as he followed.

'Oh, sorry,' said JT. 'It's all over town how you fell out of a treehouse, yeah. Come on, the Beast is at the back waiting for you.'

'KIT-KAT,' bellowed Jimmy from the other side of the shed. It took only a few large steps, then he'd scooped her off her feet in a big brotherly hug like he'd done many times over the years. 'Hey, how's your bloody form, sneaking in the other day and not sayin' G'day?'

'Put me down, Jimmy,' she cried out, with her arms locked in place.

'Not until you gimme a kiss on the cheek for old times' sake.' She kissed his cheek, and Jimmy put her down. 'You've gotten heavier, from what I remember.'

'Nick off.' She punched Jimmy's massive biceps that wouldn't hurt butter. 'How's Nora and the twins?'

'Brilliant. Still love 'em to bits. You grew up while you were away.' Jimmy patted her head like a small child.

'Don't mess the hair.'

'When was it ever *not* messy,' said Kyle, who'd always

adored her wild windy appearance. 'Here Jimmy, Kat's shout.' He handed his brother a beer.

Kat peered around the workshop, as Kyle winced inside. *Was the place good enough for her?*

It was just a work shed, but Kat saw things many didn't. He followed her line of vision to the car panels hanging off the wall. *Bugger*—he'd forgotten about the spray-painted panels his brother put up. The artwork was covered in dust and cobwebs. Did he dare ask her opinion?

Did he need it?

'My word, girl, your uncle's trained you well. Cheers.' Jimmy took a deep mouthful from his can. 'So, you're restoring Frank's ol' ute, eh?'

'I'd like to. Uncle Frank would love to see her restored.' She approached the ute at the back of the workshop, caressing the side panels with her fingertips. 'Hey, the dents are all out.'

Kyle tried to stop smiling at how she always saw the details.

'Yep, Kyle's been busting his butt on that thing since…' Jimmy asked Kyle, 'What time did you wet the bed to get in here this morning, bro?'

'Four o'clock he told me,' said JT, polishing the side of the back tray with a rag before he leaned over the back. 'We've been working on this for days. We gave the engine a complete overhaul, yeah. Then the boss worked on the steering, so you can drive it easier with your sore wrist and stuff. She's got new brakes and we've ordered a new set of white walls, but in the meantime, you've got these new tyres to kick around, yeah. But she is A1 mechanically sound.'

'Yep, then Kyle goes and beats up on the poor ol' thing,' said Jimmy with a laugh. 'He's been working on it, gettin' them dents out.'

'Wow, you guys have done so much. Thank you,' she said to Kyle.

For a moment Kyle lost his ability to speak, giving a half-shrug as he leaned on the back of the ute. 'We've only just found out how sick Frank really is. I understand why you're doing it.'

'Thank you,' she whispered, as tears glistened in her eyes. 'It means a lot to me and Uncle Frank.' She took a deep, shaky breath as if to compose herself.

She was overwhelmed, and it took everything inside him to not hold her and tell it would be okay. But he couldn't make false promises to her, especially about Frank. 'What have you got planned for Frank's day out?'

'What else, we're going fishing tomorrow.'

'Frank would like that. He used to make us swear to never share the secrets of his sacred fishing spots.'

'Frank took us out fishing a lot after Pop died, he did a lot for us,' said Jimmy. 'Who are you going with?'

'Aunty Bea and my daughter. I want Uncle Frank to teach her to fish like he did with me.'

'Besides tomorrow, what else have you got planned for the ute?' Kyle asked her.

'Nothing. The doctor said Uncle Frank would need a few days to recover before we can plan the next outing.'

'Well, I've ordered the paint and the rest of the parts, they should be here in a weekish. If you don't need the Beast, why not drop it off Saturday week and I'll work on it over the weekend?'

'Really?'

'I should have it finished by Sunday night, Monday at the latest.'

'I'll help too, yeah,' said JT, putting his hand up like a kid in school. 'No need to pay me, boss, I'll volunteer, I wanna see this beauty repainted and in schmick condition, yeah.'

'Does that mean I have to come in too?' whined Jimmy. 'Of course, I'll be here. You'll need someone to supervise you mob. I also wanna be there for the big reveal when Frank sees her all repaired. We'll have a big barbie.' Jimmy raised his beer in the air. 'I'll volunteer my services as master chef for the cookout on Frank's FJ.'

'Count me in, yeah,' said JT.

'Guess I'd better clean the barbecue for that,' said Kat. 'I'll help you guys with this, too.'

The three mechanics stared at her with arched eyebrows.

'Hey, I happen to be handy with tools, I just need direction that's all.'

Kyle laughed at her. 'Good to hear you're still the little apprentice.' It was Frank's pet name for her.

She grinned at him with that shine in her eyes he would

watch all day, if he could. *Damn it.* 'What are you planning to do with the interior?'

'I've already got the leather coming in for the seat and side panels. I just need to get a match on the colour for the roof. The original materials are no longer produced…' She pulled out her mobile phone and took photos of the interior. 'But I did find another dashboard that's crack free. Should I invest in a liner for the back tray or a mat?'

'Mat,' replied the three men.

'Okay then, I'll try and have it ready for Saturday week, and I'll help you guys.'

'Yep, we'll always need someone to make the coffee for us,' teased Jimmy.

'I'm sure I can switch a kettle on and I'll even supply lunch.'

'You're on,' said Kyle, amazed how easily she was always able to slide back into his world like it was yesterday, because they never had a tomorrow. She never allowed it.

It was a shame he was used to that.

Nine

In Uncle Frank and Aunty Bea's backyard, stood a simple square shed with a sloping roof. It had four swinging wooden front doors, with enough internal room to house two vehicles. However, inside, it told another tale…

To the right of the shed, it was standing room only for the large ute. Starting from the back wall it held a rack containing all the tools you could ever need, hung like a piece of sculptured artwork. A collection of repainted kitchen cupboards made up the workbench, with drawers of mismatched handles. It was an eclectic artwork piece of furniture used in the everyday storage of assorted nuts, bolts, screws, and nails.

Repainted rectangular school lockers stood in a line containing gardening tools, cleaned and oiled. The back corner held the drill press, the sanders, band saws, and vices. It was a working shed known to fix every day, ordinary things that Kat liked to make into the extraordinary. This was a place where conservatism was left outside, and inside the creative imagination roamed free. It was everything Kat loved and lived for.

She'd spent days in this shed getting it in order, and she was now ready for business—just the way Uncle Frank would've liked it. With the last swipe of the wood oil, she polished the wooden bar that ran along the right side of the shed.

As a child, Kat had found the slab of wood lying around in the weeds amongst a junk pile the owner didn't want. So, Uncle Frank helped her drag the massive slab of wood home, hanging out the back of the Beast's rear tray. That same day, they'd created a frame from scrap metal, added odd panels of stained glass squares, and turned it into a bar that still stood today.

From that first project, and every summer following, this shed had evolved with Kat finding and creating new unique pieces to add to the atmosphere of the ultimate man cave. Vintage photos, old tin store signs and assorted retro memorabilia hung on the walls. Barstools were made from welded car parts, and the couch was created from the rear seat of Uncle Frank's old FJ Holden.

Outside, the front of the FJ stood against the wall, and if you lifted the bonnet, you'd find the engine gone and a barbecue in its place.

They had lounge chairs made from recovered car seats, coffee tables from car tyres with antique hubcaps protected under glass. There were empty oil tins made into lamp stands, spread around for lighting. A chandelier, created from bike chains and rims, was suspended from the ceiling, and shone better than any disco ball.

All made by Kat, adding to the layer every year.

Uncle Frank's bar was the envy of many a man who entered.

She couldn't wait to show him, now it was returned to its former glory.

'Mummy,' cried Kaytlyn from the open shed doors, where the Beast was parked. 'We have a visitor.' Dressed in a purple tutu, she dragged Kyle inside.

Kat gasped for air, like a fish floundering on the side of a dry creek bed.

'This is Kyle. He says you two were friends when you were little, like you were with Aunty Wendy, huh?' Kaytlyn then frowned up at him. 'You're not going to destroy my treehouse like Mummy did with Aunty Wendy, are you?'

'No.' Kyle chuckled as he squatted onto his haunches in front of her. 'But I can help your mother fix it.'

'You bet.' The child's eyes shone as wide as her smile. 'Mummy can't do too much coz of her wrist.'

Kat cleared her throat and found her voice. 'Kaytlyn, does Nanny Bea need a hand for dinner?'

'On my way, coz Kyle's staying for dinner.' With a rustle of her tutu's many layers, Kaytlyn skipped the path to the house.

'I like the tutu, it's quirky. You can tell she's your

daughter, she reminds me of you at that age.'

Kat blurted out, 'Why are you here?'

He held up her credit card. 'I brought this back. You'd left it on my desk. I thought you might need it.'

'Oh, thanks. Forgot all about that.' Oh no, she didn't do that on purpose, did she? Like a girl's ploy of leaving her purse behind for the guy to find and return. 'Did you use it?'

'Yeah, I bought myself a jet ski, a set of gold-plated tyre rims and a massive subwoofer stereo system that takes up the entire boot space,' he said with a straight face.

'Bull.' She laughed, and his grin grew. 'Beer?' He nodded, and she moved toward the safe space behind the bar.

'I haven't been in here since…It'd be over a year.' Kyle scratched the back of his head with a frown, then smiled. 'But it wasn't like this. You wouldn't have been able to help yourself. Not even a week and you've already done your customary tornado-tearing, holiday cleaning spree.'

'Uncle Frank asked me to.'

'I should pay you to come and clean my shed.' He sat at the bar and turned her drawing pad to face him. 'What are you working on?'

'I got a job today.' She placed his frosty beer in front of him, where he had always sat in summer. Back then it was paddle pops and sodas they sipped through straws, while the grownups drank beer and manned the barbecue.

He grabbed his beer with a nod. 'Cheers. A job, huh? When, where, doing what?'

'Mrs Sternston wants me to do a monthly window display for her.'

'I'm sure you'll make her store shine. I swear it's been the same display since forever.'

'Think it'll shock the locals? It's not too much change for them, is it?'

'It'll get them curious, which is what Mrs Sternston would want if you're doing her window display.'

'That's true, I just need to attract the locals…' She tilted her head at the design she'd been working on. It was autumn, heading into winter down south, yet here, it still felt like summer. So doing the usual seasonal displays weren't suitable this far north, when they only had a wet and dry season.

'I'm sure you'll find something suitable,' Kyle said.

He always did that, gave her the right type of effortless encouragement that made her smile.

'So, what are the other jobs?' Kyle asked.

'There's the prospect of running the odd craft class from her store, if I want it.' That would mean time on preparations and advertising, which she didn't have when she didn't know how long she was staying. 'I'm also meeting Jenny—'

'Who?'

'The hospital's new head nurse. She's asked me to work on a tender proposal for the upgrade of the Nurses Quarters. I don't know how long that'll take, so I'm not depending on it.'

'Government contracts are slow. I work on the cars for their local representatives.'

'Look at you sounding all posh.'

'I'm a businessman, babe, I've gotta be.' He winked at her over the rim of his beer as he took a drink.

The wink made her blush, being called babe made her heart warm, and his smile weakened her knees, she had to grip the bar for support. Not good. 'I also got the supplier's deal for some new paint for the hardware store. That place hasn't changed at all with the way they sort their shelves. Hey, do those old guys still play cards there—'

'The ones' you called the outback mafia, after watching *Goodfellas*?'

She shrugged her reply, they'd watched that movie many times together.

'Well, they can't smoke in the pub anymore,' said Kyle, 'so they go there and have a coffee, a cigar, play a round of cards, and bitch about the weather and politics.'

'They drink coffee?' She didn't remember seeing any coffee machine in the hardware store.

'We're pretty sure they slip a good swig of scotch or rum into their coffee mugs to keep them happy, and not get into trouble,' he said with a chuckle. 'Did the Flynn brothers hassle you to vote for their movie marathon?'

'Michael did. What's the go there? Considering it was advertised on the side of a buffalo.'

'Michael nominates all these fancy foreign films you need to read more than watch, and Paul wants cheesy action comedies.'

'Does anyone vote?'

'Not enough to make a final decision, and that pair keep changing their minds, so it'll never happen.'

'Must be a tough decision, or you're a tough crowd to please.'

'Hey, I heard about the chalk paint.'

'I didn't think kid-friendly designer paint was your thing. Don't you deal in metallic spray paints? Have you painted anything new?'

'I'm about to paint a big red piece of junk, shortly.' He pointed toward the silent paint-faded ute parked in the driveway.

She gasped in mock horror. 'Where's JT when I need him to back me up?'

Kyle chuckled, sharing his sly-tequila smile that made her stomach spin. 'Nora was talking about it at home, she wants to paint the twin's rooms.'

'Well, you can tell Nora she can get it from the Flynn Brothers on Saturday when the first shipment arrives. She might want to be quick to order because I think most of it's presold already.' Kat was pleased to be getting a commission on future sales.

'Wow, you move fast, don't you? Not even in town a week and already working.' He paused with his beer can halfway to his mouth. 'It sounds like you're settling back into the place.'

For how long?

The way he looked at her, he had to be asking the same question. A question she couldn't answer.

'I'm keeping busy.' She leaned against the wall, putting the bar and distance between them.

'You're always busy, what's new there?'

'With Uncle Frank's list of jobs, the ute, fixing this house—sorry, Uncle Frank says I've got to call it home.' She said, shrugging at Kyle, 'I've got a fair bit to do.'

'Like what?'

'I have a treehouse to repair—'

'That you fell out of.' He chuckled.

'Smart arse, it broke away because the wood and ropes were rotten. It's a good thing it was us and not the kids.'

He laughed at her. 'You still bite back quick, don't you?'

Mummy. Kyle. Dinner's ready,

' bellowed Kaytlyn as she tore into the shed. 'Come on, Kyle, Nanny Bea says you've gotta come now or it'll get cold, and she hates her food getting cold.' She grabbed Kyle's hand and dragged him outside. 'You get to sit right next to me.'

'I'm honoured,' said Kyle as they walked out of the shed.

Kat turned off the lights, at a loss for words. How was she going to eat dinner when her stomach felt like the inside of a tumble dryer on full speed? She could be polite, and they could be friends. Just friends. Maybe?

*   *   *

'The end,' said Kyle, seated on the couch beside Kaytlyn, while Bea and Kat were in the kitchen. Kyle closed the picture book and passed it back to Kaytlyn, who smelt of strawberries and fresh soap. Even her pyjamas had a tiny tutu. 'Is it bedtime?'

'Yes.' She sighed, hugging the book to her chest.

'What's wrong? Didn't you like my reading?'

'No, you did great, better than Mummy—don't tell her that.'

'It'll be our secret.'

'Do you keep secrets?' Kaytlyn asked, with wide, sparkly blue eyes.

'Why, have you got a secret?'

'I don't know if it's a secret,' she mumbled, playing with the soft ruffled edge of her tutu.

'We can call it a non-secret.'

'I like that,' she said, smiling at him.

'So, is your non-secret about the book?'

'Kinda. I like this book the most because it's about a princess who has a mummy and daddy. Mummy calls me princess.'

'I believe I've heard the term *the tiara-less tutu-loving princess* bandied about.'

'That's me,' she said with a straight back, chin up, and a wide smile, minus a tooth. 'Mummy says it's my pet name. Do your mummy and daddy call you any pet names?'

'Not that I can remember.'

'Why not?'

'My mother was sick and died when I was seven, and my dad died when I was fifteen.'

'How?'

'From a freak accident in the old mine where he worked.'

'So, you had no mummy and daddy?'

'My brother looked after me, he was twenty-two. We still live in the same house we've lived in since we were babies. Now my brother has his wife and their two children living there, too.'

'Like one big happy family. You're lucky to have the same home and a big family.'

'I am.' He also used to want the same, a family of his own, but that dream had been left stone dead in a dusty ditch with other unrealised dreams.

'Did anyone help look after you and your brother after your mummy and daddy were gone?'

'Well, your Nanny Bea and Poppy Frank came and helped us out for ages, Frank was my dad's best friend. Your mum skipped school and caught a bus to stay with us.' Kyle wasn't sure if he should've mentioned the part of cutting classes. 'It was the longest your mum ever stayed in town.'

'Did Mummy bring ice cream when you were sad too?'

'She did.' At that time, he'd locked himself away from everyone, but Kat came for him. She'd climbed through his bedroom window in the middle of the night, straight from the bus station, and held him.

She was there when he'd needed her the most. Showing up without ever being asked, to stay by his side while he mourned the loss of his parents. Kat had volunteered to help and gave so much support when he was fifteen. So why hadn't she been there for him many years later, when he'd prayed she would show up—but never did?

He'd hated her for deserting him.

Could he ever forgive her?

'I'm going to help Mummy when Poppy Frank leaves us too,' Kaytlyn said as she traced the cartoon family on the book's cover.

'I'll be there to help too,' he replied without a thought. Why did he insist on punishing himself?

Because he owed her.

Kyle wouldn't have coped without Kat being there when his father had died. Against all his better judgement, he'd already forgiven her for not being there when he had needed her the most.

'Teeth and bedtime, Kaytlyn,' said Kat, leaning against the kitchen's doorframe.

'Goodnight, Kyle. Thanks for reading me the story.'

'You're welcome, night Kaytlyn, sweet dreams.' She was a cute kid, Kathryn should be proud.

'Night, Mummy.' Kaytlyn hugged Kat in the doorway.

'Want me to tuck you in?'

'No, it's Nanny Bea's turn tonight.'

'Well, goodnight my tiara-less tutu-loving princess,' Kat

said with a bow.

Kaytlyn giggled as she curtseyed, holding out the edges of her tutu. 'Goodnight my magnificent Mummy, I Love you.' She reached up and hugged Kat around the neck.

'Love you too.'

Kyle grinned at the closeness of mother and daughter, then frowned for intruding on their private family moment. Family wasn't for him anymore. Not when he'd been delegated to the support role of the relative on the sidelines of family life forever.

He jumped from his chair, eager to leave. 'I should head off, too. Thanks for dinner, Aunty Bea.'

Aunty Bea came into the lounge room and gave Kyle a hug. 'My pleasure. You must come back again soon. It's like old times, isn't it, when you boys visited every weekend for the Sunday roast? Just so you know, our door is always open to you and your brother, remember that.'

'I will, thank you, Aunty Bea.'

'I'll walk you out,' said Kat at the front door.

Nearby, Kaytlyn giggled as she skipped up the staircase, with Aunty Bea laughing behind her. Kyle hadn't seen Aunty Bea this happy and spritely in a long time. Guilt twinged between his shoulder blades for not visiting sooner. Had he been too busy to visit the people who were like family?

Outside, Kyle stared up at the silhouette of the towering tree near his twin cab ute. 'I meant it when I said I'll give you a hand in fixing the treehouse.'

'Are you sure?' Kat said.

'Yeah. We spent a fair bit of time in there as kids.' Every summer they hung out up there, camping, making up scary stories, then making out in their late teens. They'd shared so much history, but it'd been cut off so suddenly, it had created a yawning gap between them.

Kyle turned and faced her with the need to ask her hundreds of burning questions. He had so much to say to her, but she looked so fragile, he couldn't make things worse for her. Especially when she had, not only the responsibility of Kaytlyn, but now she had Frank and Bea as well.

'Um, thank you,' Kat whispered, wrapping her arms around herself.

'For what?'

'For wanting to help fix the treehouse and the Beast, but mostly for putting Kaytlyn's mind at ease. I overheard you guys talking, and I'm aware it's been bothering Kaytlyn with Uncle Frank's...' She stopped and stared at the ground, wiping her face.

'Hey—' Her tears made his throat ache. Again, without a second thought, he wrapped his arms around her and held her to his chest—it was like standing in a dream. Her soft hair against his cheek, her light fragrance, fresh and fruity, with a touch of floral spice. It was her signature scent of summer.

'Thanks.' She took a shaky breath, stepping away from him, wiping at her tears. 'It built up, sorry.'

'Don't be. Are you okay now?' He wasn't. Damning his

heart to hell, almost damning the woman before him. All those emotions he'd buried a long time ago were now wide awake, screaming to hold her, to kiss her, and to tell her how he felt.

Yet, he could never tell her back then, and he certainly couldn't tell her now.

Or was that the familiarity of their past talking?

'Yep. Thanks, I guess I needed that,' she said, standing back from him.

She was always stepping back from everyone.

He should leave too. For good.

Kyle sighed, sliding his hands into his jeans pockets. He couldn't be that much of a bastard, not when she was going through so much on her own. They could be friends, and right now Kat needed a friend. He put his palm on her shoulder and said, 'If you need anything, and I mean anything, anytime, you call me, okay?'

'Thanks.'

Would she?

'And, um, thanks for the hug too.'

'I reckon I'll call this the house of hugs, sorry, the Home of hugs.' He chuckled to himself, relieved to see her smile.

'Yeah, why's that?'

'Aunty Bea and Kaytlyn, who's an incredible kid—'

Kat coughed, and her eyes widened, blinking rapidly at him.

Did he say the wrong thing? 'I was just giving you a compliment for being a great mum to a cute kid.'

'Um, thanks,' she said with a shy smile, and if it wasn't dark, he'd swear she was blushing. 'Coming from you, that means a lot.'

Huh! Well, that made his night. 'You know, I've never had so many women hugging me, all on the same night, in the same place.'

'Consider yourself lucky.'

He'd like to get lucky—but he had a girlfriend he was avoiding, while standing in the dark with his ex.

'Well, I'd better head in,' said Kat.

It was like she'd read his mind—they used to do that a lot. They knew each other so well back then, were they really total strangers today? 'I'll see you Saturday week with lunch?'

'Sure.'

He climbed into the driver's seat of his standard ute. 'I hope that's service with a smile?'

She shrugged.

Yeah, Kat wouldn't have too much to smile about these days, not with what lay ahead of her. 'Have a good time fishing tomorrow.' Kyle couldn't remember the last time he'd put a line in the water himself.

'I will. Drive safe,' she said, waving.

'I will, it's the other drivers you have to watch out for. Hey, try not to destroy any letterboxes driving that beast around,' he called out, reversing down the driveway.

'Prick!'

He laughter echoed as he drove away. It'd been a great night, maybe they could be friends again.

Ten

'Hey bro, whatcha doin', where ya been, what's the goss?' Jimmy asked, cuddled up with Nora on the couch.

'Nothin, nowhere, nothin' to tell.' Kyle closed the front door, grabbed a beer from the kitchen fridge and dropped into his well-moulded armchair like he did every night.

'You missed dinner,' said Nora. 'Sorry, there's not much left over after the mob.'

'I already ate, thanks,' Kyle mumbled, sipping his beer.

'Yeah, where? At the pub?' Jimmy asked.

'At Aunty Bea's place,' he replied as casually as he could. 'I went there to give Kat her credit card, she left it at the workshop. I knocked on the front door and there's Aunty Bea demanding I stay for dinner.'

'Aunty Bea's a great cook, her Sunday roasts are the best. Huh, it's been a while…' Jimmy frowned at the coffee table as he scratched his head. 'Hey, how is she?'

'Happiest I've seen her in ages having Kat there, she

adores Kaytlyn.'

'What's Kaytlyn like, is she like Kit-Kat?'

'She's a lot like Kat. She wears these tutus that make you laugh.' Kyle chuckled to himself. 'I also saw that chalk paint you wanted, Nora.'

'You did?' Nora suddenly sat upright, eager for his answer.

'How?' Jimmy asked, with a cocked eyebrow over his beer can.

Kyle shrugged, trying to not make a big deal out of it. 'Kaytlyn made me draw on her walls with her. The kid's got talent, she's well advanced for her age.' He'd enjoyed sitting side by side with Kaytlyn, drawing on the wall. They drew cars together, and he taught her about shading. It'd been a long time since he'd drawn anything.

'Do you know if Kat can draw?' Nora asked.

'She was more into structural images for making things, like plans.'

It was Kat who first gave him paper and pencils, and they'd draw side by side in the treehouse. He'd do sketches of mystical creatures from imaginary worlds he'd only show to Kat. Back then, his pictures were always in black and white, until she introduced him to colours.

He hadn't picked up a paintbrush or done anything remotely creative since the summer she'd left. Somehow, he'd become the opposite to everything he missed about their time in summer. There was no more play, no more summer art, no more hiking. Kyle did nothing but work.

'Emelia rang and wants you to call her,' said Nora.

'Yeah.' Kyle frowned at the TV.

'She's called three times.'

Kyle rubbed his eyes, he didn't need this. 'I'm gonna take a shower.'

'Aren't you gonna call Emelia back?' Nora asked.

'Has he ever,' mumbled Jimmy.

The house phone rang.

'I'm in the shower,' said Kyle, hightailing it down the corridor.

'You know, it's probably Emelia, *again*,' called out Nora.

'Then don't answer it.' He closed the door to the bathroom and turned on the shower to drown out the noise rattling his brain.

There was a knock on the bathroom door and Nora yelled out, 'Kyle, Emelia's on the phone and wants to talk to you.'

'I'm in *the shower*! Tell her I'll speak to her tomorrow,' he yelled back.

'You know she's my boss, right?'

'I'm not listening.' He shoved his head under the stream of water.

'Well, buy me an answering machine to screen your calls, I'm not your bloody secretary.'

'*We love you, Nora*,' he sang out from under the hot water jets, his voice echoing off the tiles. It usually worked. Nora had been part of the family forever as Jimmy's first and only love.

Kyle used to think he had the same. Once.

He frowned as the water washed over his tired shoulders. He needed sleep, but his mind wouldn't stop. What was he going to do about Emelia? He was booked to take her out to dinner tomorrow night—to propose.

It was the first time he had a girlfriend while Kat was in town. A girlfriend who wanted to be in a long-term relationship with him.

He wasn't allowed to have a long-term relationship with Kat beyond the summer holidays—according to her rules. The same rules, every season, that they'd remain just friends while she was away. As per usual, he followed them and said nothing about what he really wanted, too scared he'd lose her if he ever did. And he still lost her by keeping silent.

It's obvious she'd moved on, starting her own family as a mother to a great kid, which was something he could never give her.

Where was Kaytlyn's father? Did the guy hurt Kat so bad his daughter never talked about him? What sort of arsehole would let Kat bring up a child on her own?

Then again, Kat had a habit of putting restrictions on people to stop them getting too close to her, so she wouldn't get hurt. But he'd never hurt her.

It's a shame she'd hurt him.

Eleven

Kat parked the Beast in the driveway of a small cottage near the hospital. It was devoid of lawn, pot plants, or anything to give it that lived-in appearance of a home, reminding her of a vacant rental.

The train whistled in the background, mimicked by the kite stretching its wings to effortlessly circle overhead in the endless rich blue. It was like a perfect summer skyline, except this was winter. This dry season's glorious weather was perfect for doing something—anything, but this. 'It's just coffee. I'm just helping out a mate who's more of a mate to my uncle.'

Kat closed the driver's door with ease. 'Huh?' She smiled as the warm sensation spread inside her. Kyle had fixed it. Who was just a friend. He was that familiar face that carried a familiar feeling, like the familiarity of this countryside that surrounded her. It was comforting.

Yet she was missing something else that should've filled

the cold hard-edged pit of loneliness inside. It was always best to stay busy to help her forget who and why.

If she hadn't booked the Beast in for a spray-paint for Uncle Frank, she could avoid Kyle for the rest of her stay in town.

Her boots crunched on the gravel drive as she grabbed the toolbox from the back tray. She balanced a small plastic container gingerly with her sore hand as she approached the front door.

'Morning,' said Stewart, opening the door before she knocked. He was handsome, with the sun highlighting the honey flecks in his eyes and in his hair. So glad he wasn't wearing that stupid baseball cap.

'Morning. Here, this is for you.'

'What's in the container?'

'Chocolate cake, Aunty Bea made it for you.' Aunty Bea was more excited over this visit than Kat, and wouldn't let Kat cancel. No matter how many excuses she'd tried, Aunty Bea kept cutting her off.

'Thank you. You know, I'm usually inundated with all these home-baked goodies all the time, but when I wanted something, I couldn't get anything, anywhere,' he said, leading her to the kitchen.

How many women were cooking for this guy?

She put the toolbox down on the kitchen floor that was exceptionally clean for a bachelor's house. *Did he own an apron too?*

'What?'

'Did you clean this, or do you pay someone?' Considering his hands were spotless and softer than her own, she guessed he paid someone.

'Cleaner. It's part of my contract with the hospital, and being on call, I'm hardly ever here to mess it up. Why do you ask?'

'Bachelor pads aren't usually this clean. I have to ask, do you own an apron?'

He laughed, and it made her smile with him. 'God no, I can't cook. I microwave or live off hospital food. Are you questioning my masculinity here?'

She grinned with a shrug, heading to the back door to work. 'I have my coffee white, no sugar thanks. Is this the door?'

'Yeah, it's—'

'It's sticking from the humidity.' She swung the exterior door a few times, spotted the problem on the base, then opened her toolbox to search for the right tools.

'Who taught you to fix things?' Stewart asked as he manned the fancy coffee machine, it was the only thing standing on his kitchen counter. There were no pictures on the wall, no magazines, no opened mail, not even a set of keys lay on the side bench by the front door. There was nothing to give this place a lived-in look, except for a batch of white doctor's coats hanging in the living room doorway.

'Uncle Frank trained me. I used to go everywhere with

him when I was a kid.'

'Frank's a handyman?'

'A builder,' Kat said. 'He used to manage the building contracts for Government housing in remote regions of the Territory. His business got huge too, until he sold it to enjoy semi-retirement as a handyman who likes his fishing.'

'Did you go with him to the big contracts?'

'I stayed for school holidays to get away from boarding school.' It was a time she'd lived for, feeling that same swell of excitement whenever she spotted the small town through the bus window. The smell of pure, fresh air, looking forward to the freedom of her hikes to enjoy the abundance of beauty in the wildlife. Working with Uncle Frank, there were many drives of discovery, searching for billabongs during their lunchtime fishing breaks that lasted all afternoon. It was a time of no pressure, of not wearing what was in style, no buses, classes or exams. Free from all responsibilities and city living pressures.

How could she ever recapture the essence of that sensation again?

'So, you learned your way around the toolbox from Frank?'

And Kyle, he'd taught her a lot too. 'Uncle Frank used to call me his little apprentice, still does. Whenever I'm renovating and have an issue, I'll call him for a solution, no matter the problem.' Who would she call in the future? She frowned while she worked on the back door.

Stewart steamed the milk as the room filled with a wonderful rich scent of coffee.

'I hope you'll enjoy it,' he said, passing her a steaming cup.

She sniffed the air and murmured, 'Mm, that aroma is divine. I used to love walking past the coffee shops in the city, with their freshly ground beans.'

'I miss everything about the city.'

Did she? Kat sipped her coffee and rolled her eyes. 'Ooh, that is liquid gold, good sir.'

'I may not cook but I can make coffee.'

'I'm impressed. So, dare I ask what brought you to this town?'

He faltered. 'Um, my father runs a small medical practice here, while I manage the hospital.'

'Wow, father and son team?'

'Not like that.' He frowned, wiping a palm over his face as if to regain his composure. 'I'm like you, this place isn't home. Although I didn't do boarding school, my parents divorced when I was young, and my father came out here.' His frown faltered again as he cleared his throat. 'Anyway, as soon as my contract expires, I'll be heading back to the ER.'

'Busy places.'

'I worked in one for years before coming here. I miss that adrenaline rush where time shifts so fast, you walk inside on a Monday, blink and it's Friday.'

She remembered the rush all too well. Did she miss it?

'This place would be a real change of pace from the one you're used to, huh?'

'That's for sure.' He took a deep breath, and with a wince, he said, 'Okay, I also got told to work on my bedside manner.'

She grinned at him over her coffee. 'No way?'

'I stuffed up in the city, on this patient—not medically—I told this idiot to stop drinking and smoking. I just didn't realise he was a close friend of the head of the hospital board.'

'What happened?'

'My ER chief suggested I go hang out in some country hospital to gain more of an all-round experience and learn how to deal better with people. My father hooked me up here.' Again, he frowned. 'Anyway, my ER chief has already agreed to take me back, with a promotion.'

'Congratulations.' Stewart had just set down his set of rules. Just like she used to say to Kyle every summer, which was to never expect anything more than the time she was staying in town. Nothing was permanent with people or places. 'So, have you learned to deal with patients better?'

'Except for you—'

'I've already said sorry.'

'Okay then, for the record, in the city they gave us a uniform so we didn't have to think or bother with what we were wearing on shift. We'd show up, change, and deal with the masses. Here...' He sighed, leaned against the kitchen counter and crossed his dress shoes at the ankles. 'I'm working on anything from kids with colds, then jumping into helicopters to attend cattle station crash sites, to being a medical examiner for crime scenes. I wouldn't get that kind of experience in the city, even though the hospital's building is bigger than this town's main street.'

'You don't like it?' Kat asked, squatting as ladylike as she could, to work on the back door. It was the first time she'd felt self-conscious while playing the part of a Handywoman.

'I'm ready to go back. I miss the conveniences of the city, and the anonymity.'

'Me too. Everyone knows everything around here.' Although she was still surprised how only a few knew how sick Uncle Frank really was.

'Do you get everyone trying to set you up with their cousin, sister, niece, and great-granddaughter too?'

'No.' She laughed at him. No one ever hit her up or set her up in this town, because she'd always been a part of the Kat and Kyle show. They were like a black and white rerun that picked up where it left off in the last episode that replayed on TV all summer long. Kind of like the five-day international cricket matches no one watched, but they were always playing in the background somewhere. *No, they weren't like that*—or were they?

'There, problem solved.' She opened and closed the door a few times, listening to its whispering glide across the floor.

'That took you less than five minutes.'

'I'm good, and so is this coffee.' She slid the wood planer

and wax back into the toolbox and sipped her coffee.

'You enjoy teasing me about my inabilities to do things as a male.'

'I do not.'

'Yes, you do.'

'How?'

'For a start, I don't know how to fix things,' he said, pointing to the back door.

'You mend broken people. I can't do that.'

'Ah, but I'm not handy around the house.'

'Most people are like that these days.'

'Okay then, why did you ask if I owned an apron, if you weren't suspicious of my masculinity?'

'Well, I was wondering—'

'I happen to do some things exceptionally well as a man.'

'Yeah, like what?'

'Like this.' He cupped her face in his super soft hands, pressing his soft lips to hers and kissed her, long, slow, and gentle.

Not expecting that, Kat opened her eyes, there was no meshing of teeth or tongue in a lusting hunger, but a slow and sensual seduction with his mouth. She closed her eyes and savoured the dance of his lips against hers, as the heat slowly rose like an electric blanket that never got quite hot enough in the middle of winter.

He pulled her closer, their bodies pressed together as her palms slid over his shoulders, admiring his musky aroma with the undertone of sterilising chemicals. It reminded her of the hospital, the wide corridors, the shiny floors, and the cold off-white room her uncle was trapped inside, on a bed, surrounded by beeping machines.

She pulled back just as the phone rang.

'Stuff-it! I was getting into that,' he murmured with a croaky voice and glassy eyes. 'I've got to… umm…' He just stood and stared at her while the phone rang.

'Answer the phone,' she said, with a sudden need to visit her uncle, even if it was just for five minutes. She could just pop in and check if he needed anything else for their fishing trip later today. Would they let her take him out earlier?

'Ah, yeah…the phone.' Stewart stepped back and bumped into the corner of the kitchen bench. He did a half turn, caught the chair he'd knocked over and grabbed the door frame next to the bench. Letting out a deep breath, he answered the relentlessly ringing phone.

Kat touched her tender lips. It was a nice enough kiss, but it wasn't in her top ten personal category winners. She took a sip of her coffee to wash away his flavour and packed up her tools.

'That was the hospital. I have to go, I'm sorry.'

'The joys of working on call.' She smiled at him over the rim of her cup and took another mouthful. 'Thanks for the coffee, and the kiss.' She gave him a gentle peck on the cheek, then grabbed her toolbox.

'Okay then, I'll walk you out.'

The phone rang again, and he scowled at the thing.

'I'll find my way. You are a man in demand, Doctor.' She waved at him from the door as he gave her a sorry shrug. She wasn't upset over the interruption. It's not like they could get attached to each other when he wasn't here permanently either. She never got attached to anything anymore except her daughter, because her daughter never rejected her.

Besides, it was just a coffee and one kiss. She wasn't sorry for the kiss, even if it brought up the wrong memories, but she was also used to driving away—and did.

Twelve

Inside the town's small supermarket, in front of the sandwich bar, Nora and Wendy stood side by side, staring out the front window. Music from the fifties filtered through the aisles, occasionally interrupted by a price check query over the speakers. The front automatic sliding doors opened and closed with the constant flow of shoppers, allowing fresh air to mingle with the scents of fresh fruits, vegetables, and barbecue chickens.

Emelia slid a group of bridal magazines into the front rack alongside other glossy covers. 'What are you two doing?'

'We're on a break. You didn't just put those second-hand bridal magazines on the rack, did you?' Nora asked. Beside her, Wendy rolled her eyes as both women slid their hands inside the large front pocket of their matching work aprons.

Emelia gave a tiny shrug, smoothed down her dress, and stood beside them to stare out of the window. 'Don't tell me that silly water buffalo is being a nuisance again.'

'Hey, did you see the Kimble's had a baby girl?' said

Nora. 'I bet they're relieved.'

'I swear they're making their own softball team,' said Wendy.

'Ick, babies.' Emelia screwed up her nose. 'What are you two gawking at?'

Wendy pointed across the road. 'Kat's doing the craft shop's window display.'

'You know, I've never seen that store window change,' Nora said to Wendy.

Emelia shrugged. 'What's the fuss over a shop window, I do ours.'

Wendy and Nora screwed their noses up at their current window display of canned baked beans, stacked into a small pyramid as this week's special.

Emelia pointed and asked, 'What does she think she's doing, putting a chair there? Mrs Sternston doesn't sell furniture. That's silly.'

'Everyone knows Mrs Sternston sells the materials that Kat used to re-upholster that chaise late last night,' replied Wendy.

Nora nudged Wendy as she said, 'You didn't fall out of any treehouses, again?'

'Nope, we're grounded, literally.' Wendy grinned wide.

'Must be nice having Kat back.'

'It is. She's still the same person, only a mother now.'

Nora tilted her head, squinting at the scene across the road. 'You know, it's like a fancy corner of a lounge room.'

'She's showing what you can do with the materials, colours and textures the store sells, as well as advertising what Kat does.'

Emelia screwed up her nose until it almost touched the window. 'What? Hang up bits of material? It looks silly.'

'She's an interior decorator, or is that designer? Whatever, I get them mixed up,' said Wendy.

'Bah,' scoffed Emelia, 'obviously, she isn't any good or she wouldn't be here doing up a local shop window now, would she?'

Nora frowned with Wendy, who said, 'Kat's won awards, and her scholarship to go to art school to become an interior whatever she is.'

'If she's that good, how come she's not doing it as a full-time business?'

'She did. Still does, I think?' Wendy said. 'Kat told me she sold her share of her first business to purchase her first unit, then flipped it to buy her first investment property, so she could hang with Kaytlyn.'

'Who's Kaytlyn?' Emelia asked.

'Kat's daughter,' replied Nora. 'You know, it's got an unusual spelling to it.'

'She gave it all up for a child?' Emelia screwed her face up as if she'd sucked on a sour lime.

'Kat loves doing up those places. You should see the before and after shots of the last place she leased. She brought some stuff with her so she can work from Frank's shed, and you have to check out her candles—they're divine.'

'Why? When we sell candles here.' Emelia pointed to aisle five.

'Not like these,' said Wendy. 'Kat made them to help sell her places, to create an atmosphere. Her clients loved them so much, she sells them. You should see her website.'

'Whose?'

'Kat's,' replied Wendy, while Nora rolled her eyes. 'It's got a gallery showing off her art pieces she makes from people's old furniture.'

'What Kat did to Frank's shed is amazing, all made from scrap materials,' Nora said, staring out the window. 'You know, my caveman hubby will only let me do up the house if he can do up his man cave first.'

'Jimmy would never move from inside his cave if he had one. Hey, we should get Kat to teach us what she calls herself…' Wendy waved her hand in circles. 'An upselling-recycling-repurposing, whatever.'

'Huh?' Asked Nora and Emelia.

'Kat uses second-hand furniture she finds on the side of the road, restores them, decorates her houses with them, then sells them as separate items. If they don't want her eclectic pieces when she flips an apartment, she ships them off to this gallery who sells them for her. She's quite famous in those arty-crafty circles.'

Emelia frowned. 'I've never heard of her.'

'Well somebody must,' said Wendy, 'because she runs

an annual craft class on how to do this whatever-stuff. It's booked out months in advance. Kat's like a proper mumpreneur.'

'Typical Kat, ten projects on the go at once. No wonder her uncle calls her the whirlwind,' said Nora, chuckling.

Emelia sniffed and inspected her manicured fingernails. 'Second-hand furniture in a gallery, *puhleese*. Sounds like a lot of silly nonsense to me.'

Kyle stood behind the three women, listening to their conversation. It wasn't like they were hiding it, with their voices bouncing off the windows, and he'd been standing there for ages waiting for service. 'Actually, it's a clever way for Kat to make a living, doing what she loves, while bringing up a child on her own.' He had to admire her for it.

'*Kyle*?' Emelia smiled so bright it was like someone had flipped on the light switch. She skipped to his side, clung onto his arm, then smacked her heavily painted lips against his cheek. 'What are you doing here, are you here to see me?'

He wiped the layer of lipstick off his cheek. 'Sorry, flat-out with work. I'm just here to pick up the lunches for the boys, my turn today.'

'Silly me, I forget how busy you are. Are they ready?' Emelia frowned at the two women.

'I'll get them,' said Nora, walking behind the sandwich counter.

Kyle peered through the window. 'Anything new happening on Main Street?'

Emelia screwed her nose up at the shop across the road. 'Someone is trying to create art from scrap material and an old chair. I've never heard of such a silly thing.'

'Whatever, it is arty,' said Wendy.

'Art comes in many shapes and forms, it's all in the way you look at it.' Just like Kyle couldn't stop watching Kat working on her window display. It was her drawings he'd seen on Frank's bar, now come to life.

'I didn't know you were interested in art, honey?' Emelia asked.

Nora scoffed, carrying over a small box. 'Pft. Haven't you seen Kyle's artwork hanging up in his workshop?'

Kyle pulled his arm free from Emelia and reached for the box, rolling his eyes at his sister-in-law.

Emelia asked, 'What? You're not talking about those old car bonnets and odd car doors with those silly cartoon characters, hanging from the roof, are you?'

'You did not just call them silly cartoons,' warned Nora. 'You know, they're fantasy art pieces. Good thing Kat didn't hear you say that because she'd tell you off.'

Kyle patted his sister-in-law's shoulder. She may be a tiny thing, but she was very protective of family. 'It's okay, Nora, that was a long time ago.' *A long, long time ago.*

'Didn't Kat enter your artwork into a competition without your knowledge?' Wendy asked Kyle. 'You won that airbrushing equipment thingy.'

'You'd just turned sixteen,' said Nora. 'We were all so

proud, you know.'

'Why don't you do it now, Kyle?' Emelia asked.

Kyle frowned down at the lunches as he checked over the order, keen to leave this entire conversation. 'I don't have the time, work comes first.' He certainly wasn't going to tell Emelia he'd lost his inspiration because his muse had deserted him.

'*Emelia, phone call line one,*' cried the voice over the loudspeaker.

'I'd better get that. I'll be ready for dinner at seven, I can't wait.' She pulled his arm down and kissed his cheek.

This time he grabbed a napkin from the box and wiped off her smeared lipstick from his cheek. 'Um, yeah right.' He couldn't get excited like Emelia, not when there was nothing inside but that all too familiar cold empty well. 'I'd better get these lunches back to the shed.' *Next time I'll pay JT to do the lunch runs.*

'Kyle, do me a favour?' Nora asked.

He stopped by the front doors, so close to freedom. 'What's that?'

Nora approached with a brown parcel in hand. 'Can you drop this lunch off on your way through, it's been sitting awhile.'

'Who to?' He put the wrapped lunch into the box amongst the rest of the food.

'It's for Kat, she's forgotten to pick it up, and you know we can't leave the store to deliver it,' said Nora, with a tight-lipped grin and shiny eyes.

'If she's that busy, she might need a drink too.' With his back to the meddling pair of women, he grabbed a certain drink as he smiled to himself and walked outside.

*   *   *

Her back to the outside world and with hands on hips, Kat inspected her window display. She hadn't dressed windows since her part-time job doing downtown department stores at midnight while attending design classes during the day.

Back then, she had to stick to their strict branding code and follow the window designers specific floor plans that matched new catalogue releases. Today, she worked to her own plans, to help Mrs Sternston promote her extensive, uncatalogued material collection that was like a forgotten part of a library. Kat could spend weeks discovering secrets within the material reams crammed inside the racks that ran from floor to ceiling in this shop.

Someone tapped on the window behind her and she jumped in fright. It was Kyle.

It was the scene of a surreal moving picture of a silent world behind glass, where Kyle stood and smiled at her, just like he did in her dreams. Her heart expanded to fight the lump in her throat as the nerves tingled in her fingertips. But it was those eyes, with their intense clarity that shot straight through to her soul, warming her all over, just like summer did every single day.

He waved a brown bag at her.

Oh man, lunch.

She gave a nervous giggle, rolled her eyes, and slapped her forehead with the heel of her palm. Her pantomime for forgetfulness had him shaking his head, while laughing at her as she met him on the sidewalk. 'Are you the supermarket's new delivery boy?'

'I do it occasionally to keep in touch with the little people.' He handed her the paper bag.

'Thanks, I forgot, and I forgot to order a—'

'Drink?' He held up a juice mix.

'Wow, they still make these? It used to be my favourite.'

He looked at the ground as if to hide his sly-tequila smile.

'Thank you.' She opened the juice bottle as he handed her a straw. 'Look at you, all decked out with the gadgets.'

Kyle stepped back to the edge of the sidewalk with their backs to the road and faced the window display. 'Have you finished?'

'Only just now. What do you think?'

'You're asking a mechanic what he thinks about fabric?'

'I'm asking you. Not some random person off the street—'

'We are street side, sweetheart.'

Her heart rolled over into a pile of creamy mush, like a

puppy in a soft flowering field on a spring day. 'You know what I mean.' If only her brain and body would get it together and remember the guy was a friend. *Just friends.* 'I'm after your brutally honest opinion, using your critique's eye for artistic creativity. Please?' She waved her hand at the shop's window area, where she'd created a scene worthy of a magazine—and her social media accounts.

She'd chosen her colour palette from the surrounding environment. Gumnut greys, local lobelia blues, dusty grevillea reds, olive eucalyptus greens, and flowering wattle yellows. All of the lovely colours synonymous with the outback.

It started with a ream of grey linen rolled across the floor for a mat, below a silver-framed script covered chaise. Beside it stood a pile of books wrapped in assorted paper, coded to the same colour palette.

A pale wattle yellow, large knit throw was draped over the chaise's edge among a few faux fur cushions. Black and white printed fabrics were mounted into assorted picture frames creating an artistic collage in the background.

Bunches of local eucalyptus leaves were mixed with bright bush lemons, adding a citrus twist to an empty birdcage. It sat beside thick candlesticks made from old lamp stands, whitewashed to blend. They rested on a tallboy with its many drawers covered in different materials, again sticking to the colour palette.

'Hey, are those lights from the hardware store?' Kyle

pointed to the ceiling where she'd suspended individual industrial light bulbs. They were covered in conical lampshades, again made up of different colours to match the palette.'

'Yep, I made the shades.'

'I use those lights for working on cars.'

'You don't say.' It's where she'd gotten the idea from.

He playfully nudged her with his elbow. 'You always did like blending the industrial into household furnishings.'

'It's my signature style, so they say.' She could blame that on Uncle Frank, hanging out with him in his shed over the summers.

What she needed now was an honest opinion, one that mattered—Kyle's. 'So, tell me, what do you think?'

He shrugged and stared at her window display, his head leaning to the right. 'I like your clever mix of colours and textures, using our local scrubland as your inspirational palette. It's a bit conservative for your taste, isn't it?' He glanced at her sideways.

'Wow.' She grinned at him, surprised and impressed he'd worked it out. 'Being my first work for Mrs Sternston, I decided to tone it down. Remember, she hasn't changed the display in ten years.'

'Breaking in everyone gently, huh?'

'Yep.'

'Didn't want to go for the major wow factor?'

'No, the *oh-my* sigh factor. Don't worry, I'll work my way up to it.'

'Well, it's a stylish use of colour to give people ideas on how easy it is to upgrade their surroundings. It's conservative, yet looks good.' He looked up and down the street, then leaned towards her. 'Hey, tell no one I said that, I'm a guy with a reputation to keep up.'

'I'm grateful for the honest opinion, coming from the grease monkey.' She pointed at his stained jeans hugging him in all the right places, while trying not to drool over the grey t-shirt that stretched across his chiselled chest. She had to squeeze her hands into fists, fighting the temptation to slide her palm across those enticing contours. *Just friends.*

Kyle balanced the box to one side and patted his chest. 'That's boss grease monkey to you, thank you.'

'What, you Tarzan—me Jane, considering your brother is the caveman.'

'You'd be no good as Jane,' Kyle said, laughing, 'not when you fall out of treehouses.'

'Not nice, mate.' She stared up at him with mouth wide open in mock shock, but he only laughed harder.

'So, what are you up to now?'

Kat peeked at her mobile's screen, then slipped it back into her pocket. 'I've got half an hour to kill. I'm waiting on the van to arrive with the first delivery of chalkboard paint.'

'How were you able to get that shipped in so fast? The train isn't due again until next week, and it's at least seven days by road freight.'

'I have connections in high places, you know.'

'You called someone you knew to deliver it? Who?'

'Guy, he makes it. He's doing an overnight drive-by on his way to see his brother, in a very diverted tour that includes Kakadu National Park. I must show Kaytlyn the park.' It was so close, but did she have time? She'd prefer to spend any and all the time she had with Uncle Frank before he left—in between school, work, and her list of things he needed doing around his home.

Kyle scuffed his boot on the lip of the sidewalk, giving her another sideways glance. 'Is he your boyfriend?'

Was Kyle jealous? He shouldn't be, he had his own girlfriend, who she never wanted to see—Kyle with another woman would kill her. *Just friends.* 'Guy is a close friend who's gay. We met in art college and shared shed space together.'

Kyle grinned as if with relief.

'Well, thanks for your honest opinion and for bringing my lunch. I'd better leave you to it, I'm sure your team are eating the rubber off the tyres by now.' She needed to get away and try to put a stopper on these unwarranted emotions and memories bubbling inside her.

'Where are you eating lunch?'

'At the park, I want to catch Guy and show him where the hardware store is. I haven't sat outside and had lunch in ages, and this is great weather.' She never had the time to stop, always working to make money; even while Kaytlyn slept, she worked. She had no one to share the responsibility, except now with Aunty Bea, who helped a lot.

'Me neither, I'll come with you.'

She peeked at him over her shoulder. 'But—'

'The boys can wait a little longer. Besides, I can't remember the last time I ate lunch away from the shed, it'd make a nice change.'

They used to goof off together all the time during summer. Even during his apprenticeship, she made sure he took a lunch break so they could sit and talk. 'What about Emelia?' *Hello, we're standing in the middle of a small town where everyone knows everything.*

A frown fleeted across his brow. 'It's just lunch—hey, since when were you ever worried about what people thought.'

'Since I became a mother.'

'Really?'

'People are very judgemental about young single mothers.'

'I'm not judging.'

He never did. Kyle had the gift of accepting her many faults. He also used to hold her, calming her internal storms, and made her world feel better. But he also let her go…and their time of forever ended in never. 'I don't think—'

'That spot under the tree looks good. You'll have a clear view of your mate as he drives in. What kind of car does Guy drive?'

'A retro pink VW Kombi van. It'll have surfboards on top.'

'There is no surf in the Territory unless you count the waves we get with cyclones. Most normal people try to avoid those and the crocodiles.'

'Guy doesn't surf, he just likes the look.' She giggled with a shrug.

'I'm sure we won't miss it in this town. Surfboards are a rarity. Good, there's no water buffalo around to hassle us for food.' He chuckled as he escorted her across the park.

'The wandering water buffalo sharing birth announcements?'

'Yeah, the Kimble's had a girl, they'll have enough kids to start their own softball team soon.'

'So I've been told.' *Many times.* 'Hey, what is the story about that water buffalo?'

'Cecil is our town's mobile billboard. You know the kids at the school feed him at lunchtime.'

'Do they? Kaytlyn's never said anything?'

'Probably so as to not freak you out. You weren't much for animals, were you?'

'Ah, hello, it's big, with horns.'

'Cecil's tame, the kids brush him down while sharing their lunch with him, and draw all over him.' They sat on the bench and ate their lunch, watching the town's world pass by. It was so different from her life, hustling a living in the busy city. Yet, eating lunch here was something they used to do together all the time, in this place that held so many freedoms she used to share with Kyle. Now here they were, talking with that same ease, and why not? After all, they were friends first and always. Maybe?

Thirteen

'What are we doing here?' Emelia asked, screwing up her nose.

'It's the only place left to get a feed on a Friday night,' replied Kyle, escorting her into the local pub, where the aroma of beer and grilled meats mixed with deep fried food and assorted Friday night perfumes. It wasn't train-week, so only a few groups sat scattered in the simple rustic dining room. Kyle gave a nod and a wave to the few seated locals. A ruckus of rough voices blended with rock music, filtered in from the busy front bar.

'Hey, there's Jimmy and the family.' Kyle strolled over with Emelia dragging her feet behind him.

'Kyle, what are you doing here?' Nora asked in wide-eyed surprise, while Jimmy dropped his head to inspect his palms in his lap with sudden interest.

'Have you guys ordered yet?' Kyle pulled out a chair for Emelia as he sat next to Jimmy.

'We were just about to,' replied Nora. 'Weren't you

going—'

'That's great, the restaurant mucked up our booking.' Kyle passed Emelia a simple laminated bar menu, then stole a sip of coke from his niece's glass across the table. 'Are you kids getting the nuggets, as per usual?' Thomas grunted, and Jamie nodded. 'Don't they have roo brains and goanna-tongue that they can blend for you to suck through a straw?'

'With wild magpie goose gizzards for dessert,' said Thomas with a grunt, over his sister.

'Ew,' complained Jamie, screwing up her face.

'You look nice tonight, Emelia,' mumbled Jimmy, while Nora half-rolled her eyes.

'Thank you. It's nice that *someone* noticed.' Emelia smoothed down her black dress, with her lips pressed into a tight line, she glared at Kyle.

'Is that a new dress?' Nora asked.

Kyle shrugged. 'Ah, sorry, is it new?'

'Um, wasn't your last new dress black, too?' Asked young Jamie.

Kyle winked at his niece, grateful to her for the save. 'Let's order, I'm starving.'

As they ate their meals, a large burst of laughter carried in through the side door, and they all turned to see the pub's newest arrivals.

'Hey, it's Kit-Kat,' said Jimmy, sitting taller than the others at the table. 'So that's Kaytlyn, huh? You're right, bro, the tutus make you laugh.'

'I'd love a tutu too, they're fun.' Jamie pointed to Kaytlyn, in her rainbow coloured tutu over her jeans and boots.

'I don't,' grunted Thomas, his cheeks bulged with food and his lips were smothered in tomato sauce.

'Who are those two men with Kat?' Nora asked. 'They're not from around here.'

'They're Kat's mates from the city, Guy, and his boyfriend, Quentin,' replied Kyle, checking out the newcomers as the adults at his table all swivelled to face him. 'What?' Did he have to re-explain he'd had lunch with Kat in the park, in front of the world?

'Thank you for doing the lunch deliveries, and I'm glad you *finally* had a lunch break away from the work shed,' said Nora grinning at him, very pleased with herself.

'Here, here. But next time bro, go earlier, so JT doesn't faint from starvation,' Jimmy said, playfully shoving Kyle in the shoulder.

Kyle hadn't felt like playing in a long time, not like he wanted to now. It'd been a long time since he'd sat back in the sunshine, sharing lunch and a conversation. A brief moment where there was no talk of tomorrow, free from all weight-bearing responsibility. A feeling he only got with Kat.

'Why are they here?' Asked Nora, being Nora.

'Guy makes that chalk paint, he brought it out for Kat,' replied Kyle.

'It's here, *yes!*' Thomas grunted, fisting the air with his fork.

'Great, there goes my weekend watchin' the footy,' mumbled Jimmy, sipping his beer.

'What are they doing, and why are they all covered in paint? In public. On a Friday night. They look silly.' Emelia gasped in horror. 'She always was a messy girl with her wild hair and dirt, wearing those cut-off shorts all the time.'

Kyle liked Kat in those cut-off denim shorts and her wild, rich auburn hair. It was a look he used to admire, especially while following her denim-clad backside on their many hikes throughout the region. She looked even better tonight, in torn jeans and a long-sleeved white shirt, splattered in coloured paint. Her wide smile and shiny mint-green eyes were undeniable. She was his stereo of summer songs, full of words he could think, write, paint, but could never ever say aloud, because he was only a spectator adoring the charm of her chaotic ways.

Jimmy nudged him in the ribs and he frowned at his brother. 'What?' He then realised Emelia was watching him stare at Kat.

One look at Emelia's icy blue eyes and he knew their life was a masquerade. He rubbed his chest, where his hidden scars were the walls surrounding his ribcage, protecting his fractured soul. A blackened soul that used to hold a kaleidoscope of colours that shone for another, the only one.

Why did Kat come back?

*　　*　　*

'Look, Mummy, there's Kyle.' Kaytlyn pointed, and her paint-splattered tutu bounced as she ran to the table.

'That's just great,' Kat mumbled under her breath. Kyle and his whole family were watching her. Worse—the girlfriend was glaring at her like she wanted to claw her intestines out and make a noose from them, to hang Kat from the ceiling fans.

It turned her heart to ice to see Kyle with another woman, then it rushed in a fiery green-eyed burst of hatred towards Emelia. Kat clenched her teeth and her stomach knotted, but she had no right to be jealous.

Not when the Kat and Kyle show was over a long time ago. He'd rejected her, and it was obvious he was where he wanted to be—living a life without her.

'I can't believe this weather is your winter, it's like our southern summer,' said Guy, fanning himself at the bar as he checked out the dining room. 'Oh, yummy mummy, our tutu-loving princess has taste. Who is that man?'

'Kyle and his brother, Jimmy, with his family.' The shattered pieces of her heart squeezed out all essence of happiness it had ever held, while staring at Kyle and his family. She used to be a part of that crowd, a part of their celebrations, where her spot used to be beside Kyle. Now she was an outsider, for he had another sitting in her place, Emelia.

Kat squinted at the blonde, blue-eyed beauty who was

neat, tidy, and feminine. She was everything Kat wasn't, and must be what Kyle needed. He was forever off-limits now, and she hoped Emelia would make him happy and give him everything Kat couldn't.

'Go fetch the child and that man she's speaking with,' Guy said, nudging her in the shoulder. 'Quentin and I will get the order.'

'Great.' She took a deep breath, pasted on a smile, and patted her paint-tangled hair. Raising her daypack on her shoulder, she buttoned the oversized old shirt. She wasn't properly dressed for the dining room, especially the way Emelia was glaring at her—like she always had as a child.

But Kat was all grown up now, and raised her chin and walked tall.

Until she stumbled on the carpet.

'Careful,' called out Kyle, catching her before she hit the table and sent their drinks flying.

'I'm good.' Kat wanted to snatch the ice from their drinks to drip on her hot face while standing under the ceiling fan. Guy hid his face in his palms, only to peek at her through the gap in his fingers, with Quentin laughing beside him. *Great.* 'Hi, guys. Hey, that's not Jamie and Thomas, is it? You guys got big.' She used to babysit them with Kyle.

'They go to my school, Mummy, they're a few grades above me,' said Kaytlyn. 'Jamie also wants a tutu, we have to talk Nanny Bea into making more.'

'I'll let you do the hustle on that one, kiddo.' She patted

her daughter's hair then faced Kyle's date. 'Emelia, isn't it? Hi, remember me?'

'Still messy, I see.'

The bubble of jealousy still stirred inside her chest, it took everything to not snap back. Instead, Kat stepped away from the table, grabbing Kaytlyn by the shoulders, ready to bolt.

She should leave.

But she just couldn't help herself.

'I'm sorry,' Kat said as sarcastically as she could, 'but, I didn't check my dark mirror when I left my inner prude in the back of the black closet. But I did remember to wear shoes to get service in a pub. I'm sure there's a country song written about that.' She pointed to the air where country music floated in from the front bar with men yodelling to the chorus.

Emelia scowled at her with her chin raised, smoothing down her black dress while Kyle squirmed in his seat. *Uncomfortable much, cowboy?*

'Are you aware paint is for walls and not clothes, silly? Lose the manual on that one, did we?' Emelia sniffed at the air as if Kat reeked like a city garbage truck after a long weekend fermenting in the summer heat.

Kat now wanted to go in for the kill. 'Thank you so much for noticing—'

'We've been having a paint bombing party,' said Kaytlyn, her wide eyes matching her eager smile.

Kat slammed her mouth shut tight. What was she doing,

having a sledging match with her daughter present? Again, she tried to steer Kaytlyn away from the table.

'Paint bombing party?' Jamie asked, while her brother beside her busily shovelled food into his gob.

'It's the coolest thing. We fill up water balloons with all these different coloured paints. Then we play cricket with them to splat them across this big board. Then we use it on drums and make music while splatting paint everywhere. Sometimes, the grownups use darts, but we couldn't find any.'

'I think we're capable of making a mess without them.' Kat again patted Kaytlyn's shoulder and tried to get the kid away from this crowd.

'You're throwing paint at each other?' Jamie asked.

'That's cool,' mumbled Thomas with a mouthful of food.

'And then,' said Kaytlyn with wide eyes, 'we emptied the smallest supermarket on the planet of all their water balloons and garbage bags.'

Kat giggled at the supermarket reference, Nora snort-laughed as Emelia scowled. Emelia always was a sourpuss, sitting at the shop counter, painting her nails.

Kat glanced at Emelia's pampered hands, feeling her paint-spattered fingers curl in shame as she hid them behind her back. *Not fair.* Most of the time she didn't think twice about her hands, they were merely the tools of her trade, but tonight she made a mental note to give herself a manicure.

'Are you gonna clean up with those garbage bags?' Jimmy asked Kaytlyn.

'No way. We're gonna wear them to slide across these panels to blend the colours.'

'I've never heard of such a silly thing,' scoffed Emelia.

'We used to do it in Uncle Guy's shed in the city. I'm not lying, am I, Mummy.' Her chin in the air, Kaytlyn faced Kat for confirmation.

'No, honey, we do it to achieve a unique paint blend—'

'To create original masterpieces for backdrops. Aaaand because it's too much fun not to,' interjected Guy, flicking Kaytlyn's tutu as he joined the group. 'Hi, I'm Guy—Ooh, you're gorgeous, and those eyes are amazing,' he blurted out to Kyle.

'Manners, Guy, we don't want to scare off the general public,' Kat said, elbowing him in the ribs. Kyle dropped his head, shaking it, while Jimmy playfully punched him in the arm. 'Guy, this is Kyle and his brother Jimmy, who are mechanics. Although, for a pair of grease monkeys, you boys scrub up all right.'

'Listen to you losing the valley-girl vocals for the yodelling local lingo, and swapping your handbags for a daypack like a girl scout,' said Guy, tugging on her day pack.

She rolled her eyes at Guy. She'd missed him, but the backpack was suitable for her walking around all the time. She'd done it to make a point, to teach Kaytlyn about being prepared in the bush. 'Thomas and Jessica are the twins I used to babysit, and this is their magnificent mother, Nora.'

'And who is this?' Guy asked.

'Emelia,' Kat mumbled, as if she'd stepped into a pile of steaming cow pats that swallowed her shoe.

'I'm Kyle's *girlfriend!*' Emelia's words rang around the room.

It used to be Kat's title, and hearing those words spoken by another just shattered Kat's soul.

'Okay, I have the pizzas coming, two bottles of champagne for the crew that counts. One bottle of tickly tequila for shots. A case of beer for Frank, and a bottle of lemonade for Kaytlyn. Is that going to be enough?' Quentin stopped reading from the receipt in hand. 'Oh, hello people of the outback.'

'They're not aliens, Quentin.' Kat tried to not giggle, feeling alienated herself, yet grateful for the interruption.

'Are you sure?' Guy pointed to Emelia with her eyebrow arched in disdain. 'She is wearing a little black dress in an outback pub? Do they do that? I was expecting thongs, shorts, and sweaty singlets.'

'Yes, I mean no,' stammered Kat, trying not to snort-laugh. 'We've got Wendy coming over, so we should get another two bottles of wine.'

'What do we pour for the cute doctor?' Quentin asked.

Guy tapped Quentin's chest with the back of his hand. 'Babe, he's been dubbed the Hot-Doc, get with the program.'

'Stewart is bringing his coffee, I hope,' replied Kat with a shrug, and caught the fleeting frown from Kyle. 'I think we have enough, Guy. We don't need to spend all that hard-earned paint money at once.'

'Pft.' Guy flicked his wrist in dismissal. 'That's why we have receipts, to claim it on this business trip. Oh, we should fetch some scotch for hot shots in the Hot-Doc's coffees,' he said to Quentin, who dutifully returned to the bar.

'Hey, what have you lot got planned for tonight, sounds like a big one?' Jimmy asked.

'More paint bombing,' said Kaytlyn. 'Mummy calls it another one of her impromptu parties, we used to do it in the city.'

'It sucks that you're here,' whined Guy, giving her his sad puppy-dog pout. 'We miss your impromptu parties. Everyone's still talking about your farewell rooftop toga party.'

'The what party?' Jamie asked with her brother giving a questing nodding beside her.

'Toga party,' replied Kaytlyn. 'We ran around in bed sheets and partied on the roof of our apartment, and everyone in the building came. It was wicked fun.'

'Pizza's ready,' called out Quentin.

'Great, I'm starving. Nice to meet you, bye.' Guy waved and headed for the bar.

'We're sorry for disturbing your dinner,' said Kat, trying to herd Kaytlyn away.

'Pizza? Didn't Aunty Bea cook tonight?' Kyle asked Kat.

Kaytlyn ducked under Kat's arm to stay at the table. 'No, but you should see Nanny Bea, she's covered in paint and she's even wearing a tutu. You should come see.'

'Ah, they're eating dinner.' Kat wasn't sure about the extras for tonight. She wanted fun, not drama.

'They can help, Mummy.' Kaytlyn then spoke to Kyle and his family, 'You should come, it'll be loads of fun. Doctor Mannen is gonna sneak Poppy Frank out of the hospital to do an inspection on the shed—now Mummy's cleaned it up and got the lights all working. It's like a party in a proper backyard. I've never had one before.'

'Um, what? A party?' Jamie asked.

'No, a backyard,' replied Kaytlyn.

Kat's heart squeezed with icy pain. Had she denied her child the simplicities of life, like a yard to play in?

'Is Frank getting out of hospital?' Kyle asked.

'The—' Kat caught herself from saying Hot-Doc— 'Doctor is bringing him over on his break.' From the bar, Guy and Quentin waved at her, carrying pizza boxes and assorted bottles. 'Come on Kaytlyn, we have to go.'

'Mum, can we go over there tonight, pleeease?' Jamie begged Nora.

'It's been a while since we've visited Frank's, luv?' Jimmy said to his wife.

'Too long,' said Kyle, nodding to his brother.

Nora smiled and said to Kat, 'You know, it sounds like a lot of fun. If that's okay with you?'

'Sure. They can come, can't they, Mummy?' Kaytlyn asked, jumping up and down on her boots' toes causing her tutu to shift in waves.

Kat shrugged at her partying princess who wouldn't leave the table. 'I'm positive Uncle Frank would love to see you guys, then you can explain to him what you did to the Beast, because I have no idea.'

Jimmy patted his little brother's shoulder. 'I'll be happy to give Frank a full rundown.'

Kyle shook his head at Jimmy. 'You didn't even work on it.'

'Hope you've got that ol' FJ barbecue cleaned up, Kit-Kat?'

'I do. I guess I can hunt down some meat for the cavemen to burn later. We have to run. The shed doors will be open, you know where to find us.' She herded Kaytlyn out the door, unsure if Kyle would go, but if he did, he could leave that sourpuss Emelia behind.

Fourteen

Children squealed and adults laughed as water balloons, full of paint, burst all over them. Their garbage bag coveralls were severely ineffective in protecting skin and clothing.

Uncle Frank, with his oxygen bottle and tubes, sat in his FJ couch between Kyle and Jimmy. The party lights shone over the lawn where Aunty Bea played with the children, both big and small. Haloed by the industrial chandelier, Wendy, Nora, and Guy were deep in conversation at the bar, when Kat approached with the children. 'Hey, you two mothers and the fairly-ugly-godfather.'

Guy waved his champagne in the air. 'Oh, that's me.'

'We've decided to have a sleepover party in Kaytlyn's room tonight so their magnificent mummies can be home alone to indulge in a sleep-in.'

'I don't know?' Nora frowned, as her children nodded at her eagerly.

'Aunty Bea's keen,' said Kat, 'and it's purely for my own

selfish gain, because Kaytlyn will have other kids to occupy her in the morning. I've already promised to take Guy and Quentin swimming at the falls tomorrow, so the more the merrier.'

'Quentin and I bought all this new hiking gear for the trek,' said Guy. 'We can't wait to test it out and see our first proper billabong.'

'You know what? I will take you up on that offer,' said Nora. 'I can't remember the last time it was just me and Jimmy.'

'How can it be just the two of you, when Kyle lives there too?' Wendy asked, topping up her wineglass.

Guy bounced higher in his seat with wide eyes, nodding at the two women he'd been drinking with. 'Kyle can stay here.'

Kat frowned. 'What? No.'

'Yes. He can sleep on the couch. He's the twin's uncle, I'm sure he'll help look after them,' said Guy, elbowing Nora.

'What? Oh, yes—of course.' Nora also sprang higher in her seat, her head bobbing up and down at Wendy. 'I know Kyle will do it. He's great with the twins and he hasn't been on a hike in years, you know.'

'Huh? Oh! Yes, you can look after Sammy.' Wendy raised her wineglass to Guy, then grinned at Kat. 'I'll appreciate the sleep-in, thank you very muchly, whatever, happy to repay the favour in the future.'

Kat narrowed her eyes as she pointed to the trio. 'What

are you three up to?'

Stewart approached and touched Kat's elbow. 'Um Kat, I'm sorry, but it's time to take your uncle back up to the hospital.'

'Oh, no,' she whined. Uncle Frank was having a great time at home, where he belonged. Also, Stewart was growing on her. It amazed her how warm his hands were away from the hospital, and there was that slow and steady curl of heat that spread from his touch. 'Did you have a good time?'

'I did, which makes it hard to leave.' He frowned at the phone ringing in his hand. 'Sorry, I—' He took the call and walked away.

Kat chewed on her lower lip as the sorrow threatened to ruin her, watching her uncle laughing with the brothers. She couldn't complain or barter, because Stewart had warned her if he got the call they had to leave. It was part of his rules in allowing Uncle Frank's impromptu leave pass from the hospital. Strange that—when it was Kat who normally set the rules.

She turned down the stereo feeling like Cinderella's evil step-mother about to spoil their ball of rags. 'Sorry, everyone, it's time to say goodbye to Uncle Frank for the night.'

After helping Uncle Frank, they all stood around Stewart's car to bid their farewells, one by one.

On the driver's side, Kat spoke with Stewart. 'Thank you for bringing Uncle Frank tonight.'

'I'm glad to help, I had a great time. When I get my next

days off, I'll take you out to dinner or something, okay?'

'Sure.' She shrugged, it's not like she had anything else planned. Besides, how long would dinner last before he got the phone call to leave? Strange that, when it was Kat who always left first. 'Oh hey, it's my turn to say goodnight to Uncle Frank.'

'Okay then, I'll call and we'll set up a date,' called out Stewart.

'Sure.' Unsure if she would accept his offer, when Stewart reminded her of the hospital and her uncle's illness.

She walked around the car, past Kyle who arched his eyebrow at her. *What's his deal? And where's the girlfriend, Emelia?* He was just another guy who reminded her of the worst in her past, too.

'My turn, Uncle Frank.' Forgetting all her dramas, she crouched down and gave him a hug, he held her tight in his frail arms. 'Did the shed pass the inspection?'

'You've done a great job on the ol' shed, kiddo. Good to see me little apprentice still has the knack with the tools.' He patted her on the head like he always did when she was younger. 'It's good to see the bar gettin' a workout again, eh. Especially with those boys here, it's like the old gang's back.'

'Wish you could stay, Uncle.'

'Nah, I'm good, but it's nice to know life at home still goes on.' He lifted her chin to face him and said, 'I missed you not being around home all these years. I'm glad my little whirlwind's back to liven the place up again.' He gave her a fatherly peck on the forehead and she hugged him again.

She didn't want him to go.

'Now, we can't keep the Doc waiting. Dunno how he's gonna explain the paint over us.'

'We'll come and see you tomorrow,' Kat said, giving him a squeeze before letting him go.

'I'm expecting you to come up with one of the paintings you did tonight, for my room.'

'We'll be there as soon as the paint dries.'

'Only after you've taken your mates to the falls, then you can tell me all about your adventure, kiddo. Keep an eye out an' give me a report if you see any Barra in that billabong.'

'Maybe we'll go fishing there next?'

'We'll see. Ooroo you mob, keep on partying,' Uncle Frank cried out, with his arm waving out the window as the car drove away.

The small party stood in silence at the end of the street, watching Stewart's car drive down the road. Jimmy hugged his wife Nora, who held the twins as a family unit. Wendy held her daughter Sammy, who sucked her fingers. Aunty Bea hugged Kaytlyn in her tutu, and Guy and Quentin held onto each other.

Kat hugged herself, until Kyle walked up beside her and put his arm around her back to comfort her. She leaned her head onto his shoulder, inhaling his familiar aroma. With the sense of future loss, Kyle was the anchor to the storm inside her, as the tears trickled blurring her vision, she held him tight until the car lights disappeared.

Uncle Frank was a big part of their family, and all too soon he would be gone from their lives forever.

Kat took a deep, shaky breath and wiped her tears, trying to compose herself to face everyone, all wearing the same glassy-eyed expression. 'We all heard the man, let's get back to it, and we'd better get the kids' sleeping arrangements organised.' Kat hoped the children's excitement could inject the fun back into the atmosphere.

'So, I'll get the linen,' said Nanny Bea, and they all headed for the party shed.

Kat turned to Kyle, who was still holding her hand. 'Thanks for that.'

'I said I'd be here,' said Kyle. 'Uncle Frank's always been there for us.'

Not always, it's how she'd learned not to rely on anyone. 'I'd better get these kids organised.' She squeezed his hand and let go. She had to. She couldn't go back there, not when Kyle had rejected her first, and it was his rejection that had been the worst from the many of her past.

Fifteen

Kat woke to silence, cringing at the colours and light in her Aunt's guest room, trying to remember last night. After Stewart and Uncle Frank left, they'd setup Kaytlyn's room for the sleepover, then drank until the kids went to sleep. Nora and Jimmy walked home through the back paddock, and Wendy disappeared, as did Quentin and Guy.

Suddenly she realised, she was not alone in her bed, with her arms were wrapped around—Kyle.

On-no! How?

She shifted the sheets to see she was still wearing her nightgown, but Kyle had no shirt on.

How did this happen?

Kyle was meant to crash on the couch, but that's where they'd found Quentin, passed out. Kyle wanted to sleep in his car, but she couldn't let him do that, he would've suffered a sore neck, all cramped in the cab.

What possessed her to tell Kyle it was okay to crash with

her—which they did as soon as their heads hit the pillow.

As she stared at his sleeping face, handsome wasn't a strong enough word for how magnificent and peaceful he looked. Even asleep, he was still deliciously sexy.

She stroked the shadowed stubble on his jaw which accentuated his devilishly handsome features. She gazed down at his bare, sculptured chest, watching the rise and fall with each breath.

Then she noticed the scars.

Long jagged scars ran across his rib cage, and a long one ran down the centre of his chest. *How? Where? What happened?* Filled with concern, her fingertip traced their slashes etched into his skin. They spurred so many questions inside her.

She gazed up and lost her ability to breathe. He was awake, staring at her with his intense stare and those eyes, the colour of the rare gemstone Lapis Lazuli blue with fine gold flecks. There was a constellation within those eyes that stared straight into the deepest parts of her soul. A place where it was a sin to not love back.

His hand covered hers, holding it to his chest. His beating heart pounded strong beneath her palm, it matched her own quickening beat. Her stomach quivered, her breath stopped as he leaned in closer. Millimetres became miles as he stared at her, and time stretched to aeons as she waited. Frozen, yet warm.

His lips brushed against hers, it was just a tiny touch of heat that exploded into a pure pleasure sensation under her skin.

He stopped and stared down at her.

Her heart pounded in her ears as she sunk back into her pillow, as if sinking into the depths of heaven itself. She held her breath as if he held her universe as his lips, again, brushed hers and she was swept her away like a tiny tugboat lost in a rolling sea.

She fell with her heart first like a puzzle reconnecting, as pleasure purred and desire pushed the passion that soared up her spine. Her fingers brushed through his hair. His chest pressed to hers, lips mashed, tongues tasted, and she'd never been more alive, trapped within this perfect world.

His hands spoke words that glided across her skin, turning her mind over to places unseen. She moaned under the pleasure of his touch sending electric currents to override her pulse that ruled her reality. Chest to chest, she tasted the coarseness of the stubble on his jaw, inhaling his spice as her body craved the love felt from his hands. She held onto him, for Kyle had given them wings that demanded they fly.

A toilet flushed and children laughed as they skipped past their closed door.

'Oh no, kids.' She was supposed to be babysitting.

She pushed him away and sat up panting, her heart pounding, her ears ringing, and the fire still roaring inside. She grabbed her cardigan, and bolted for the door.

She didn't even look back.

'Hey, what are you lot doing?' In the corridor, she stared

down at the four small children she'd volunteered to care for on this tour of duty.

'We're going to get breakfast, Mummy,' replied Kaytlyn.

'Fine, lead the way, troops,' said Kat, ensuring her bedroom door was closed behind her. How close were they to crossing that line completely?

She followed the kids down the stairs and passed the snoring Quentin sprawled across the couch. She shooed the munchkins into the kitchen for breakfast, grateful they were making her focus on them and not her thoughts.

Except one—*that two-timer wasn't thinking about his girlfriend, was he?*

Fire brushed her cheeks as she dropped her head in shame. She wasn't one to talk; not when she was the one at fault for allowing him to sleep there.

How could they be friends now?

With all those feelings stirred up inside her, it was impossible to switch off, but she had to. He wasn't allowed to hurt her again—not when he'd stomped all over her heart and destroyed all her hopes and trust. Because of Kyle, she'd never dared to rely on anyone again.

There's no way she'd risk him doing that to her again. Ever. 'I need coffee—now.'

*   *   *

Kyle couldn't stop watching her. He'd been doing it all day, but only from afar because Kat had done her best to never be alone with him.

Even though they weren't together, they still worked like a team. During the hike, Kat took the lead, and he took his post at the rear keeping the children, Guy, and Quentin, between them. They finished off each other's sentences while swimming with the kids and rock climbing the secluded waterfall walls. She'd made him take in the moment, to see the things they shared with the children. From lazing wallabies, wild boar, screeching fruit bats, blue tongue lizards, and the many wild birds on the billabong, just like they'd done as kids with Frank leading them. Now he'd done it with his brother's kids and Kat's child.

Today he'd seen how in sync they were with each other. It may have been seven years since he'd hiked anywhere, but it was like he'd only done it yesterday with Kat.

Earlier, they'd waved goodbye to Guy and Quentin, who were off to explore Kakadu National Park in their pink Kombi van. Aunty Bea was at the hospital, and the kids now settled, spread across the floor. His niece and nephew were beside the finger-sucking Sammy and Kaytlyn, eating popcorn and watching a movie.

He liked this family scene; it was a shame he could never have one, except to be there as the relative on the sidelines.

The back-screen door opened as Kat took the garbage outside, and he followed. The yard was back to normal, free from any water balloon remnants, with only a few spots of paint left on the grass.

'Are you okay?' Kyle asked, leaning his shoulder against the wall.

'Sure, you?' Kat closed the lid on the rubbish bin, but it wouldn't sit and she struggled with it.

'Look, this morning…' Again, he stopped. His words were never voiced when he had so much to say to her.

'Nothing happened, okay. Don't worry about it.' She tried to be casual, hiding her shaky hands behind her back. She'd always hated confrontation as much as he did.

'But it did happen.' He grabbed her arm to stop her walking away.

'You have a girlfriend who you're meant to be getting engaged to, and they set us up,' she blurted out in a rush.

'What was a setup?'

'The whole thing, between Guy, Nora, and Wendy, forcing you to stay over last night.'

'Were you in on it?'

She arched her eyebrow at him.

'Obviously not.' Not when she was quickly warming up to a ticked-off expression he well remembered. 'How? When it was you who offered to babysit the kids to give Jimmy and Nora a night off.'

'I did, and you were meant to get the couch. Except Guy made Quentin sleep on the couch, knowing there was no way I'd let anyone—especially you—sleep in their car.'

She cared. 'But the fact remains, even with their gentle manipulations, we—'

'No. There is no *we*. There's no *you and me*. There is you and Emelia, remember?'

He didn't want to hear it, and pulled her into his chest, cupped her chin and kissed her, hard, with everything she stirred inside him.

She tasted like a sweet summer storm—the rain to his desert, still with that same untapped wildness he adored in her flavour. The softness of her curls spilled through his fingers, and he swam in her aroma like he'd done during all those summers, always side by side. Now he was greedy for the fire they used to share—the fire that was still there.

Her arms around him, chests pressing, her response filled the void that had been missing from deep within the marrow of his bones.

He had never loved anyone like this.

'*Uncle Kyle, the movie's finished,*' Jamie yelled from inside the house.

Damn. 'In a second.' He pinned Kat to the wall, both breathing heavily, with their arms still wrapped around each other. He could see that fire dancing in her mint-green eyes, and he'd tasted the passion in her kiss. It was still there.

But was it?

He stepped back from her with his palm wiping over his mouth, but her flavour was now reimprinted into his DNA. 'I've been asking myself one question since you've been back, and that is…what would it be like to kiss you again?'

He had his answer.

'I have never felt this way with anyone else, or even come close to experiencing what I feel with you. The passion we feel between us every time I've kissed you, even after all this time, it's still there—but now it's stronger. Yet, no matter how hard I tried to forget you with other women, I've never even come close to the same sensations I get with you—and only you, Kathryn.'

He turned to leave, but stopped and looked back at her leaning against the wall, her hair wild, her eyes questioning, and her swollen lips parted. Sexy, untamed, and completely uncatchable.

'I. Feel. Nothing—without you.' Just the cold iron grip from his scars, squeezing all sustenance from his soul as she frowned at him. It was a sure sign that her defences were once again rebuilding those damned walls that kept him out in the cold. 'I'm damned if I do—and I'm damned if I don't with you.'

And for the first time in his life, Kyle turned his back on her and left his soulmate behind.

Sixteen

On the warm Sunday afternoon, Kat leaned back on the picnic blanket under the dappled shade of the gum trees that lined the river bed. A lazy breeze carried a honeyed wildflower scent as it wove downstream to feed into the billabong. On the far edge, a pair of graceful black storks and grey brolgas foraged amongst the reeds, as a group of spoonbill herons waded past. Perfectly mirrored pairs of green pygmy geese floated lazily through the wild lotus lilies, their petals peeled back to soak up the sun straight into their hearts. Bright azure blue flashes came from kingfishers dipping and diving in their skilled aerodynamics as they skimmed across the watery surface. Occasionally a loud pop and a splash had them all stop and search for the cause of the sound.

'Did ya hear that, kiddo? They're here. Now, all we've gotta do is jag one,' called out Uncle Frank. He sat back from the edge with Kaytlyn beside him, teaching her how to fish for that elusive fisherman's prize, the mighty barramundi.

Aunty Bea sat on her fold-up chair near the picnic blanket and pointed at the pair. 'It's just like I'm watching you when Frank taught you how to fish at that age. She's an exceptional child, you should be proud of what you've done on your own all these years.'

'I'm very lucky to have Kaytlyn, she's a good kid.' Kat's heart swelled with love in the picturesque scene before her, and reached for her camera to capture more memories of this moment.

'Kaytlyn also reminds me of someone else.'

'Yeah, who?'

'Her father.'

Kat remained calm as she glanced at her aunt. *No, it's my secret.*

'It's obvious they're not aware of each other.'

'H-h-how?'

'I could see it when they were side by side. She has his eyes.'

Kat had seen it herself. They ate the same, they shared the same sense of humour, even their laughs were similar. She'd been amazed at how much two people who'd never met, shared so much in common.

'I believe you have your reasons, so I won't say anything.'

'Good.' Kat sighed with relief. She didn't need anyone interfering.

'But I have to say this…'

Kat winced as her aunt leaned in closer. *Here comes the lecture.*

'So, you've seen how well they get along and how wonderful he is with children, don't you think Kaytlyn deserves to know who her father is too?'

Kat frowned. 'I never knew who my father was and grew up without one.'

'You had your Uncle Frank, who has always treated you like a daughter, he still does. We both love you as our own.' Aunty Bea reached over and gently squeezed Kat's arm. 'I won't interfere, because I trust you must have your reasons for not saying anything to him, but I have to ask…'

Kat again prepared herself, because the way her aunt squirmed with hesitation, it wasn't a comfortable question she was about to ask.

'When was the last time you spoke to your mother?'

Kat scowled at the dirt, ripping up a stray wildflower. 'The day I told her I was pregnant. She told me I'd made my own bed and could wallow in it.' Kat threw the shredded wildflower and watched it fall like confetti into the dirt. Just like she'd been tossed aside by her mother, when pregnant and alone at eighteen. 'Mum told me it was history repeating itself and that I should've known better. She wrote me a cheque for two hundred dollars and said to take care of it.'

'So, my sister—'

'Slammed the door in my face and told me not to bother her again. I was too much of a reminder of what she *should* have done when someone gave her a handful of cash to get rid of her little problem.'

'So why didn't you come to us? We would've helped you.'

'I tried to tell you.' It was the truth. At the time she'd gripped that phone so tight, with tears feeding her fear for the future, but she couldn't say the words. 'I asked you both how you'd feel if I was to defer design school, remember?'

'Oh.' Aunty Bea sat back into her chair, nodding as she tucked her hands into her lap.

'You both told me how disappointed you'd be because I was halfway through my course. I was already disappointed in myself. I didn't plan it, it just happened. I didn't have the heart to tell you why, when I knew I was only going to disappoint you more.'

'So is that why you disappeared?'

Kat nodded, filled with the pain of her past, the stubbornness of her present, with a fear of the future stirring inside her.

'Those three years of not knowing where you were, worried us.'

'I didn't want to bother you.' Kat never wanted to bother anyone, and didn't want to carry the burden of disappointing anyone again.

'So where did you go?'

'To a home for young single mothers, where they taught us how to care for our babies. Once Kaytlyn was born, we ventured out into the world on our own.' Swearing to never rely on anyone again, but the sting of rejection still cut deep.

'So why didn't you tell the father?'

'I tried so many times, I could never get a hold of him. I'd left dozens and dozens of messages for him to call me, but he never did. There were no return phone calls, no letters, nothing. He'd cut me off cold.'

'That doesn't sound like—'

'Kyle.' The name rolled in a deafening echo in her ears, slamming down the lid on any feelings she held for him in a trunk, padlocked shut, kicked to the far corner beneath the bed, with the key tossed into the sea. 'Kyle had the responsibilities of the house, his brother, and everything else going on in his own life. The decision was mine. It was my responsibility, and I've never needed anything from him'—*or anyone again.*

'So are you going to tell him now?'

'He's supposed to be getting engaged to someone else. Can you imagine the kind of strain this would put on their relationship?' Emelia could give Kyle everything Kat couldn't. Emelia was everything Kat wasn't. Even if she was a try-hard cheerleader, Emelia was a neat, tidy, cultured, blue-eyed beauty, with blonde hair that behaved. Emelia was the epitome of femininity with perfectly manicured hands, who'd make the perfect future president of the school PTA. It's what Kyle deserved. Not some screw-up of a single mother who turned junk into junky art to make spare cash to feed her kid. Kyle deserved the order and grace he'd get from Emelia—not the chaos Kat always brought with her.

'Maybe this will be good for them too,' said Aunty Bea.

'I don't think so. I remember my stepfather's face when he found out I existed—*after* he'd married my mother. No way I'm putting my daughter through that kind of rejection. Ever. Kyle will get married and have children of his own, then he'll be too busy with them to bother about his first—'

'*Mummy!*' Kaytlyn squealed, 'We've gotta fish. We've gotta fish.'

'Come on, Aunty Bea, this is Kaytlyn's first fish.' Kat grabbed her camera and helped her elderly aunt to her feet, grateful for the change of conversation.

The air echoed with their laughter, as Uncle Frank and Kaytlyn reeled in their prize catch. Kat took photos to record this small milestone in her daughter's life. No, she didn't need to bother Kyle with this; she was doing just fine on her own.

Seventeen

Surrounded by an assortment of car wrecks, Kyle stood under the shade from the stretched canopy, near the tiny tin shed that housed their paint. The whirl of the air compressor drowned out the world while Kyle worked the spray gun, focusing on the bent, black, car bonnet.

He'd started this on Saturday afternoon after he'd dropped off his brother's children in front of their house, where he'd waved at his sister-in-law at the front doorway. He didn't want to see his brother or answer Nora's questions, so instead, Kyle drove around to where he always ended up—his work shed.

Once he'd made up his mind, he made one quick phone call, opened the tin shed at the rear of the work shed, and pulled out his spray gun and paints.

He hadn't touched the spray gun or his refined airbrush in seven years.

Seven years ago, his muse left him and he hadn't found the heart to use them…

Until today.

It took a while to get a feel for the correct flows, to find that momentum once again, by slashing paint along the side of a scrappy car.

He then dragged out a car bonnet he'd hidden amongst some old cars that had been pecked free from flesh, leaving their discarded metallic carcasses to cast shadows across the gravel.

Kyle had to bash and re-bend the panel into shape, secured it with vices to stand, and then he began.

He refused to surrender to the ache in his back, the tightness in his fingers, or the hunger in his stomach, working through Saturday night.

Jimmy found him on Sunday morning and brought him coffee and a toasted sandwich. Still, Kyle didn't stop. He didn't want to talk or think, only focus on this project.

With the smooth flow of paint from the nozzle, he applied a fine layer of green. But was it the right green? It needed to be lighter. He released the airbrush's trigger, unscrewed the paint bottle and added more ice-white to the mix, he needed mint-green.

Over his shoulder, he spotted Jimmy and JT watching him from inside the shed. It was Monday afternoon, and he had a yard full of cars to work on. Yet, it was rare for him not to be working from sunup to sundown, never stopping to put the tools down. He'd live here and work non-stop if Jimmy didn't drag him home for dinner.

Kat used to do that for him too. She'd wait at the gate and he'd rush out of the shed the second it was knock-off time, so they could watch the sunset together. She'd bring him lunch, and they'd share it in the shade of a tree, or she'd make him goof off, sunbake, swim, or stare at the stars. She used to give him a life outside of work and showed him how to appreciate the beauty of a moment, and his art. Without her, he was all work and no play.

Yet this job that stood before him, he just couldn't stop. Scared that if he did, he'd never do this again, not while the internal vision was blinding him to the outside world.

He picked up the airbrush, the air compressor kicked in, and all that mattered was the panel of paint in front of him. He saw nothing and no one, just his work.

'I want to talk to you,' bellowed out Kat with fists on her hips, standing on the other side of the black panel.

'What the—' Kyle stopped and blinked. Rubbing his eyes, he stepped back and inspected his work, then up at Kat. He glanced over to see his brother and JT still watching from inside the shed.

They didn't matter, only the woman did.

Kat glared at him in her green dress and heels, with crossed arms plumping up her breasts. The wind tossed her wild lazy curls as the sunlight captured the rich depth of the different auburns within the strands. His breath caught in his throat, making it impossible to swallow the lump, until he recognised the fire in her eyes.

'Well, hello to you too, Kathryn.' Kyle flicked off the compressor, bringing a heavy silence to the air, then he faced her with his artwork standing as a barrier between them.

'I have to talk to you.'

'Talk, huh?' From the blazing inferno highlighting her eyes, Kat was beyond talking, she was out for blood and, somehow, his head was on that chopping block. 'I broke up with Emelia.'

'That's why I'm here.'

Putting down the airbrush, keeping his back to her, he cleaned his hands on a rag. 'How do you know?'

'I'd just gotten back from the funeral home after helping Uncle Frank organise his own service, when I walked through the kitchen door and picked up the ringing phone to find Emelia abusing me.'

He frowned at her. 'What did she ring you for?'

'She's blaming me for you dumping her. What the hell were you thinking? You had a future with this woman. She wants you and says she loves you. I won't let you blow your chances on something—'

'There was NOTHING.' He threw down the rag. 'I don't love her. Not when I love you,' he bellowed at her, walking around the painted panel to stand in front of her.

She pointed at him so angrily, her hand shook. 'Don't you dare put this on me, not when she can give you something I can't. She's everything I'm not.'

'What?'

'You can't reject her. You're not allowed to reject her, not when she can give you so much more—'

'She isn't you! There is no one but you, and there is no way I'll ever reject you. I never have. It's you who has always rejected me!'

She gasped, her eyes widened, and she stepped back.

He'd hit a nerve, he could see it. He closed the gap, standing well within her hitting distance. 'What are you so scared of? Tell me?'

Through gritted teeth, she said, 'This...we can't.'

The air crackled like the spark before a summer storm, electrifying the humidity in the air, where the heat intensified and thunder rolled through them as they stared at each other.

'Yes. WE. CAN.' He pulled her towards him at the same moment she leaped into his chest, the impact almost winded him, but he wasn't stopping. With messy hunger, their lips meshed together. All that anger and pent-up emotion erupted inside, and he couldn't let her walk away, not without reminding her how good they were together.

He picked her up in his arms, her thighs latched around his body. His palm slid up her thigh, gripping that exquisite arse of hers, and she moaned in his mouth.

It was now or never—and there was no way in hell he was letting her walk away. He opened his eyes and spotted the small tin shed.

It was the longest six steps of his life to carry her inside the door. With one swipe, he cleared the bench free of tins, scattering them across the shed's floor. He groped for the door handle, never letting his lips leave hers, and slammed the door on the outside world.

Eighteen

Kat woke up with her body still deliciously tingling, and stretched lazily, with a warm glow inside her. She only got this sensation from one man. Kyle.

She sat up on the large leather couch in Kyle's office. Alone. Only the sounds of the air compressor whirred on the other side of the closed door.

She gathered the soft blanket around her and went to search for him.

Tucked in the far corner of the dark shed, shone the low spotlight of a single lightbulb. Beneath it, Kyle sat on an old wooden crate facing a piece of black, crumpled metal. With airbrush in hand, he focused on painting his canvas.

From the shadows, she watched him while he worked.

Barefoot, and only wearing his jeans, his muscles danced as he manned the airbrush fluidly, with such a fierce concentration it made his eyes glow under the light. He was obsessed with the art piece before him, lost in his own world.

Kyle was talented with his art he did for personal

pleasure and rarely shared. Unlike Kat, who sold hers to the unseen masses over the internet or at an art gallery, Kyle did his work for himself or to share as a gift truly from the heart.

Kyle turned the air compressor off and silence filled the dark shed. He put away his tools, wiped his hands on a rag and stood to stare at the work before him. His eyes shone, and he smiled that sly-tequila smile of his, the one that always made her thirsty in summer.

'Kat?'

'I didn't mean to disturb you.'

'No, I've just finished.'

'Can I take a peek?'

He nodded and stepped back, watching her approach.

She walked around and stood beside him, her eyes widened and she gasped, staring into her own eyes.

'Do you like it?'

'It's…it's…'

'You.' His hand pressed softly to her lower back as his breath brushed her shoulder where his salty, citrus-spiced aroma only added to the magic.

Kat tried to take in the details under the single light globe, where he'd painted her portrait. It was her face, her eyes larger than life, captured frozen in that one moment of time. Her naked torso was modestly covered by long lazy curls of hair, swirling around her in the wind. She stood at the top as if climbing out of a whirling twister. Lightning bolts and dark storm clouds surrounded her as if she commanded the power of the storms like a supernatural being.

'It's magnificent, Kyle.' The intricate details of each hair strand, right down to the smattering of freckles across her nose. It was powerful, captivating, yet demanding of her attention.

'It's for you.'

'What? No.'

'It's a gift for you,' said Kyle, 'I painted it on my old Monaro's bonnet. Do you remember that car?'

'I do. You used to call it your baby.' She squinted beyond the image to the bonnet. It was bent and twisted, like paper screwed up into a tight ball, that had then been reopened and made to lie flat. Now it stood with the indentations still marking it, as if scarred for life. 'What happened to that car?'

'Destroyed,' he whispered.

'Why, what happened?'

'You don't know?' He stepped back from her, frowning at her with a mixture of confusion crossing his face.

'I have no idea what happened, but I do know you loved that car.' He'd spent all his spare time fixing it, panel beating it, spray painting it. What he'd learned during his apprenticeship, Kyle practised on that car. It became a masterpiece of a muscle car, envied by many men.

'You mean, no one told you?'

'Told me what, Kyle?'

He staggered back, but she grabbed his hand to stop him slipping further into the dark.

'What happened to that car to end up like this?' She pointed to the bent metal he'd used to paint on. He loved that car.

'I crashed it.'

'What? When?'

*   *   *

Kyle stared at the bonnet of the car as the memory replayed. 'I was travelling along the main highway, when the car in front of me blew a tyre. They spun out of control and slammed into my car, which catapulted me into a tree.'

'Oh, no!' She gasped and her hand covered her mouth.

'I was in an induced coma for six weeks, in intensive care.' He patted his bare chest, covered in chaotic road tracks of scars. Even now the heat burned, crushing his ribs until it hurt to breathe. 'My chest got crushed by the steering wheel and my right leg was so badly broken, there's a plate running down the full length of my thigh.'

'Why didn't anyone tell me?' Tears blurred the colour of her eyes, as her hand rested over his scarred heart.

'After three months, they let me out of the hospital. Then it was another few months of rehab, staying at home. It took a year to fully recover. I'm okay now, just some scars, the leg gets heavy, and, um, some things will never be the same.'

'I'm so sorry.'

He grabbed her hand and leaned down to stare into her eyes. 'You really didn't know about the accident?'

'No.' She shook her head.

'I used to pray for you to show up.'

'I didn't know.'

'I thought you'd deserted me.'

She gasped at him. 'I would never—'

He couldn't stop, not when he'd been quiet for so long. 'I had believed you'd turned your back on me and never wanted to see me again. I thought you didn't care enough to show up and see me. And I hated you for not showing up.' At the time he'd cursed, cried, and mourned for her.

'I didn't know.'

'What would you have done if you had known?' He braced himself for the wrong answer.

Tears streamed down her cheeks as her hand caressed his chest, soothing the scars beneath her palm.

His heart ached for her pain.

'I wish I'd known,' she whispered, 'so you didn't have to go through that alone. I would never have left you alone.'

And he believed her.

His fingertip caught the teardrop from her dainty chin, then he kissed her cheek and held her close to his scarred chest. 'You're here now,' he whispered, hoping she would stay and share a future—but she'd never promised him before.

It's a shame he was used to that.

Nineteen

Fresh from his morning shower, Kyle jogged down the stairs into the kitchen. Jimmy sat at the table while Nora was at the sink, both dressed and ready for work.

Kyle made himself a coffee, took his seat at the table and waited for it. 'Morning.'

'Well…' Jimmy sat up as if holding court, with his hands gripping the sides of the breakfast table. 'Look at what the Kat kicked outta the kennel.'

'It's about time you came home, you dirty stop-out,' Nora said with a giggle, putting a plate of hot food in front of Kyle.

'Thanks, I'm starving.' Kyle sipped his coffee, watching Jimmy over the rim of his cup.

'Come up for air, did we?' Jimmy leaned on his elbow, wearing his big, cheesy caveman grin and said, 'You know, poor JT's scarred for life after the performance you two put on yesterday.'

'Damn.' Kyle dropped his head, he'd forgotten JT and

Jimmy were watching before he could get inside the shed. They hadn't been quiet inside that small shed, where they'd stayed until dark.

Nora took her seat at the table, between the two brothers. 'Did you two talk?'

Kyle shovelled food into his mouth and did his best to chew.

'Doubt it. One minute they're dogfighting with each other, and the next it was all combustible action.' Jimmy nudged Nora, who went red in the face, sniggering behind her coffee cup. 'It's a wonder that ol' paint shed's still standing.' The big man roared with laughter as tears squeezed from the corners of his eyes. He clutched his belly with one hand, while he slapped the table with the other.

'What's so funny?' Thomas asked, walking into the kitchen in his school uniform.

'Your father's having a joke is all,' replied Nora, wiping the tears from the corners of her eyes. 'Your lunch is on the bench. Please don't feed it all to the water buffalo.'

'What can I say, Mum, Cecil loves your sandwiches best.' Thomas shrugged, opened his backpack, and shoved his lunch inside.

'You know, we should be charging Esther for feeding her pet pygmy water buffalo,' mumbled Nora.

'Cecil's not a pygmy, he's just short,' said Thomas.

'And gettin' fat. You kids are overfeedin' that buffalo at school,' said Jimmy, chuckling behind his mug.

'Where's your sister?' Nora asked.

Thomas zipped up his backpack and hollered to the roof, 'Jamiiiieee.'

'Coming.' Footsteps thundered through the ceiling and down the stairs as Jamie rushed into the kitchen, clutching a large book to her chest.

'Are you ready to go?' Nora asked Jimmy, while passing Jamie her lunch.

Jimmy put his breakfast plate in the sink, then messed up Kyle's hair as he walked past. 'I'll open the shed, eh, boss?'

Kyle nodded with a mouthful of food.

'Jamie,' said Nora, 'you're not taking that photo album to school, are you?'

'But Muum, I need it for my school project. You said I could take it.'

'I know what I said, and that was for you to take copies only, not the originals.'

'You heard ya mother,' said Jimmy.

'But Daaad, it's for the family project for school,' begged Jamie, craning her neck back to face the big man.

'It stays home.'

'Aww—no fair.' Jamie dumped the photo album onto the kitchen table.

'Get in the car or you'll be late for school,' said Nora, grabbing her handbag. 'Bye Kyle.'

'See ya when you get there, bro,' said Jimmy.

'No worries. Have a good day, you lot,' called out Kyle

over his shoulder, as the small family unit left with a bang of the front door.

Kyle ate his breakfast in silence, staring at the old photo album. He flicked through the thick cardboard pages showing photos of his mother and father with Frank, who stood as best men at his parents' wedding.

There were photos of Kyle and Jimmy as babies, as they grew into small children, and even a few with Kat as a small child. She was part of his life way back then too.

He stared at a faded-edged photo of Kat and himself, sitting side by side on an old wooden crate. The Beast stood behind them all shiny and new, parked beside Frank's shed.

Kyle peeled back the sticky covering, took the photo out of the album and grinned at the image, well over twenty years old.

That Christmas was the year their mother had died. Kat's Uncle Frank and Aunty Bea had demanded they share Christmas together, which became a tradition because that was the year Kat stayed for her first summer holiday. She was five and Kyle was seven, smiling side by side.

Kat still had the messy auburn hair, and he clearly saw how much Kaytlyn looked like her mother, almost the same age in the photo.

He put the photo down, lifted his coffee cup to his mouth, when he glanced back at the image and froze.

'Damn!' He slammed the coffee mug onto the kitchen table and rushed from the room, leaving the pages of the photo album open. The coffee in the cup vibrated, his breakfast lay half eaten, as the slam of the front door echoed to the rest of the silent room.

But the picture was gone.

Twenty

Inside the treehouse, sitting cross-legged on the new floorboards, Kat finished screwing the final paint-splattered panels to the wall. She weaved the new curtains through the rods and measured the brackets.

A car drove up, and she peeked over the ledge to spot Kyle getting out of his ute below.

Why is he here? She'd been trying to keep busy, to not overthink about last night. She'd taken Kaytlyn to school, who was none the wiser that naughty mummy had been out all night. Aunty Bea hadn't said anything before she left to visit Uncle Frank either.

'Kat?'

'*Up here.*' She hammered the curtain bracket into place.

Kyle climbed up the new ladder and poked his head inside. 'Hi.'

'Hi, yourself. What brings you up here?' From the expression he wore, did she dare ask what was wrong?

'It's been years since I've been up here.' He checked out

the small treehouse and the new panels. 'Here, let me have a go.' He stole the hammer from her hand and continued to put the bracket in place.

Kat sat back against the far wall and got ready to pass him the new paint-splattered curtain. 'Shouldn't you be at work?'

'I needed to ask you something.' He embedded the nail in one well-aimed hit of the hammer.

Show off. She handed him the curtain rod, which he hung in place. 'Go on, say whatever's got you so bothered.'

'How can you tell?'

'You look nervous. What's wrong?'

'I am nervous.' He put the hammer down. Mirroring her cross-legged position, with his palm he wiped over his mouth, took a deep breath, and asked, 'Who is Kaytlyn's father?'

Her eyes widened, pressing her back against the wall. 'Huh?'

'You heard me, I want to know who Kaytlyn's father is— and don't tell me it's none of my business.'

'Who have you been talking to?' The only person who knew was Aunty Bea.

'No one.'

'So why the question?'

'I found this.' He held up an old photo of herself and Kyle about the same age as Kaytlyn.

She gasped, covering her mouth with her hand. She could see why he asked. It was her hair and her facial features that blended with Kyle's and his eyes, that made the child.

'Tell me, Kat, who is Kaytlyn's father?'

Fear rolled inside her like acid in her throat. With her sweaty palms she tried to still her trembling knees, as she sat cross-legged on the floor of the treehouse. 'You are.'

'You're kidding me.' He clutched his head and stared at her with those intense questioning eyes.

'No, I'm not kidding.'

'When? How—okay, I get the how, when we were lovers back then, but when?'

She tried to breathe, but her chest constricted at the thought of releasing a secret she'd carried alone for so long. 'It was our last summer, that last night we'd spent together in the back of the Beast. That was the night I fell pregnant.'

'Why didn't you tell me back then?'

'I tried. As soon as the doctor confirmed it, I tried to call you. I rang and rang, but no one answered at your house, and when I rang your work, they said you were away. I'd left you dozens of messages to call me back, but you never did.'

'When was this?'

'Two months after I'd left here. When I didn't hear from you, I'd assumed it was all over between us, and the last person I had left to turn to for help was my mother.'

Kyle screwed his face up in horror. 'What did she do?'

'Gave me a cash cheque and told me to have a nice life. So that same afternoon, I left everything and everyone behind.'

'Oh, no.' Kyle hung his head and cradled his face in his

hands.

She sat upright with jaw clenched and said, 'I moved to the other side of the country, and that's where I had Kaytlyn.'

'Where you've been bringing her up, all on your own, all these years, thinking I didn't want to know.'

'Yes.'

'That's why you said nothing when I met her. Why didn't you try again?'

'I did try again,' she said with a sneer. 'When I finally found the courage to call, I got told you were doing great and had a girlfriend. You'd moved on and I was expecting you to start your own family.'

'So after all these years, I'm a dad?' He squinted at her.

'Yes.' Was he mad at her? It was hard to read his expression, but knew she'd shocked him too.

'I'm a dad to Kaytlyn.'

'Yes.'

'I'm a father.' He stared at her with wide eyes, as if the realisation had just hit him, and he wasn't happy about it.

'Hey, I'm not asking you to take any responsibility. I don't need or want any money or anything from you. It was my decision back then to have the baby and to bring up Kaytlyn on my own. I'm not expecting you to get involved, and we don't have to tell her anything.'

'Are you kidding me?' He scowled at her. 'Kaytlyn doesn't even know her father exists'—he punched his chest—'ME!'

'I didn't think you wanted to know. My father never wanted me—'

'That's not your fault! Your mother never remembered who your father was, from a drunken one-night stand at the pub! But you knew me. You knew who I was. You knew *we were together!*' His words rang in her ears, as their voices bounced off the small walls inside the treehouse.

'I tried to contact you—'

'And you assumed it was all the same, with the way your mother treated you all your life.'

'Yes, and don't think you can waltz in and out of Kaytlyn's life when you want to, either,' she said, pointing her finger at him. 'I don't want her to ever suffer the feeling of rejection the way I did, thinking my stepfather wanted me as his child. Believing all those false promises that someone wanted to be my father, and then find out he didn't. There's no way I'll let you do that to Kaytlyn.'

'Are you *kidding me*? Do you honestly believe I wouldn't want to get involved in her life, for Christ's sakes, *she's my daughter!*'

They glared at each other, sitting cross-legged on the floor as the last of his words echoed inside the tiny treehouse.

He sat taller, shuffled closer, grabbed her by the wrists and lowered himself to look her in the eye. 'Kathryn, when did you find out you were pregnant?'

'I told you, it was a few months after I left here.'

'When? What month? What was the date?'

'It was Friday the twenty-seventh of March. I remembered the date because it was your twenty-first birthday. I rang your work, and they told me you'd taken off for a long weekend away. I hung out until the following Tuesday morning, sitting by the phone, waiting for you to call, but you never did. You never returned any of my messages. Nothing.'

'I couldn't call you.'

'I'm sure you had your reasons,' she said coldly, pulling her hands free from his.

He shook his head, wearing a pained frown that flittered across his brow. 'I'd left town that Thursday on the twenty-sixth, which was the night of the accident. It was the night I almost died,' he said in a low tone. 'I was airlifted from the crash site and sent straight to the city hospital. Jimmy, Nora and the twins drove down. No one from work or town knew we were there, because it was days before they contacted anyone.'

'That's how come I never found out?'

'Yes.' He nodded at her with such sorrow in his eyes, her heart plummeted through the treehouse floor.

'Oh, Kyle, I—I thought you didn't want to know.'

'They told me at the hospital, with the amount of damage I'd sustained from the accident, I'm sterile. I can't have kids. I thought I'd never be a father, just like your Uncle Frank. He helped me through a lot of that, to try and cope once I'd found out I couldn't have children. Now,'—he glanced up at her—'all this time.'

'Are you saying you want this?'

'My god, *yes*.' He grabbed her hands and shuffled closer, their knees touching. 'I wanted to search for you, but I couldn't, not when I wasn't whole and couldn't give you children. That's why I settled for Emelia, she doesn't like kids. Kathryn, you've given me the greatest gift I never thought possible. I love it—*I'm a father*. Can we go tell her now?'

'What?'

'Let's go tell Kaytlyn that I'm going to be her dad. I'm Kaytlyn's father.' He laughed as he hugged her.

'Um, sure, if that's what you want,' she said, unsure of his unexpected reaction.

'Let's go tell her now?'

'She's still in school.'

'Oh-yeah, forgot.' He sat back with the biggest grin on his face.

'So, are you saying you want to be involved?' She had to ask, to protect her daughter.

'Yes. More than you know, I want this. I promise I won't reject her, ever—are you sure we can't get her from school?' He pleaded with her.

'No, I want to finish the cubby house as a surprise for her today. Mind you, she's already in for an enormous surprise when she gets home.' Kat was unsure how her daughter would react.

'Fine, I'll help you finish this.'

'But you've got work?'

'What could be more important than this? I promised Kaytlyn I'd help you repair the treehouse. Hey, how did you come up with the name Kaytlyn, anyway? Nora said it's got an unusual spelling to it.'

'Um,' she lowered her head and mumbled, 'it's a combination of her parent's names, Kat and Kyle.'

'I love it.' His eyes brightened, his smile widened, and he kissed her.

'What are you doing?' She squirmed, trying to push him away.

'Celebrating. I thought we could christen the treehouse while no one's home.' He pushed her onto the pile of cushions and smiled down at her. 'Hey, you're never to get rid of the Beast, either. We conceived our daughter in the back of that red ute.' He made her laugh as he kissed her, but was she ready to give in to her dreams of a happily ever after?

Twenty-One

The day was a whirlwind, and Kyle was in the centre of it, where his feet had yet to touch the ground. He'd never been so overwhelmingly wracked with nerves over meeting a child—he already knew.

What if she didn't want him? What if he wasn't good enough for her? What if he failed her? All these thoughts rushed through his head as he paced the floor of Aunty Bea's kitchen.

'How can you be so calm?' Kyle asked Kat, sitting back in her chair, sipping her tea.

She grinned at him. 'I can tell you're nervous.'

'I don't want to mess this up. How do you do it?'

'I mess up all the time.' She giggled at him, then sobered as she said, 'You still have the escape option, to back—'

'No. We're doing this today and every day. I'm not backing out. But I'll call Jimmy soon.'

'I'm surprised you haven't told him yet.'

It still surprised him with all that had happened this past

24 hours. 'I've been busy learning.' He stood at the table covered in photo albums and flicked the pages of baby photos of his daughter. 'I've missed so much. I know I've got a lot to catch up on.'

'Don't take over.' Her voice was calm, but the warning was loud and clear.

'I want to be a part of her life…' He hesitated at the voices coming up the driveway. 'If she'll let me.'

The back door opened and in ran Kaytlyn, her dark auburn hair reflected the sun like a halo, with her pink tutu bouncing as she skipped inside. 'Mummy, Cecil the buffalo loves your trail-mix muesli bars so much, he chose me today over all the other kids in the schoolyard. He let me draw on his back—' She stopped, dropped her pink backpack onto the floor, and stared up at him with her smile so wide, it shone in her eyes—*his eyes*. 'Hello, Kyle, how come you're here?'

'Hold on,' Kat said, 'why are you feeding a water buffalo?'

'Kat, please.' He was dying here.

'Oops.' She shrugged at Kyle, then faced Kaytlyn, his daughter. 'Honey, Kyle and I have to tell you something, take a seat.' Kat put Kaytlyn into a chair beside her. 'You should sit too, Kyle. You're wearing a hole in the floor and I don't need to add tiling to my list of work around here.'

He wiped his mouth and sat down hard.

'What's wrong, Mummy? How come Kyle looks so…' She twirled her finger trying to find the word.

'Worried,' replied Kat.

'I am.' Kyle was petrified.

'Why, what's wrong? Can we fix it?' Kaytlyn reached over and patted his hand. 'Mummy's good at that, she fixes lots of things. We did the kitchen sink the other day.'

'It's not that, it's complicated,' Kyle said, looking to Kat to fix this.

'I need you to listen to what I have to say, okay?' Kat slid her arm around the little girl's shoulders and said in the brutally blunt style of Kathryn Jones, 'Kyle is your father.'

Kaytlyn sat up and stared at him. 'Is it true?'

'It's true, I only found out today. I'm your dad—daddy—your father.' What should she call him? A name he'd never thought anyone would say until today.

'How come?'

'Er—' He faltered and again looked to Kat. Had she explained the birds and bees to a six-year-old? How had she coped so long on her own? She deserved a medal, when he was already panicking after five minutes on the job.

'Let me explain…' Kat calmly explained all, while Kyle sat across from Kaytlyn in one of the most difficult conversations of his life!

'So, what do you say, Kaytlyn? Would you want Kyle as your dad?' Kat asked.

'Do you want to be?' Kaytlyn asked Kyle.

'More than anything,' he replied. 'Do you, Kaytlyn?'

The child was unreadable as she glanced at her mother.

They shared a nod, that tight bond between them, squeezing his heart. He felt like he was interfering—but he wanted to be a part of this; he didn't want to be the relative on the sidelines anymore.

Kaytlyn then turned and leaped at him with the widest smile, wrapping her arm around his neck. *'I have a daddy,'* she squealed into his ear, with a death grip around his throat.

Aunty Bea stood in the kitchen doorway with tears of joy. Even Kat's eyes glistened as he held his daughter in his arms.

'I have cousins now, don't I?' Kaytlyn asked.

'I think we'd better call them up, they'd want to know.' Kyle couldn't wait to share the news with his brother.

'So invite them over and we'll have a big family dinner to celebrate,' said Aunty Bea.

The hours flew so fast, Kyle was still spinning long after Jimmy, Nora, and the twins had gone home from their family celebration, where they'd crowded around Aunty Bea's kitchen table. He finished reading a book to Kaytlyn, and tucked his daughter into bed for the first time in his life. 'Well, that's it, sleep time now.'

'Can you stay...*Daddy*?' They grinned at each other.

'Sure, I'll hang around until you go to sleep.' He sat in the chair, holding her hand. Staring at the drawings she had on her wall, as a heaviness washed over him. This emotionally draining day had been the pinnacle in a week of surprises, twists, turns, and unexpected pleasures.

'Will you be coming back?' Kaytlyn asked, as if a little fearful.

'Sure. If you want me to?'

'You bet.' She giggled, then frowned while tucked under her covers, chewing on her bottom lip.

'What's wrong? You can tell me anything.'

'Why?'

'Because I'm your father.' He stroked her nose, noticing they were the same freckles as Kathryn's, but it was his eyes staring back at him with worry. 'What's wrong?'

'Are you going to be like Sammy's daddy? She only sees him once a month because he's busy with work and lives so far away.'

'Wendy's daughter, Sammy, from next door?'

'She sucks her fingers, but she's getting better. Sammy told me her mummy and daddy don't love each other anymore. Do you love my mummy? It's okay if you don't. I've got plenty of friends who have parents like that.'

Yes, he loved Kat but wasn't sure how she felt about him. With everything else happening so fast, the only future they'd discussed was Kaytlyn's, where Kat had stipulated that Kaytlyn came first.

He now understood why Kat was so protective over Kaytlyn, because he was the same. 'I promise to be around whenever you need me. I'd like to be around as much as possible, if you want me to?'

'Does that mean you'll follow us wherever we go?'

He frowned and caught himself, but his heart crackled like a lump of ice that was being smashed by a hammer. 'Has your mother said you'll be moving away?'

Kaytlyn's eyelids grew heavy as she murmured. 'It's what we do.' She smiled with closed eyes and whispered, 'Goodnight, Daddy.'

'Goodnight, my little tiara-less, tutu-loving, Princess.' He sat there watching her, hoping he never let her down.

How long did they have before Kat decided it was time to leave? Again.

Twenty-Two

Kat drove the Beast into the mechanics yard for its makeover that had taken weeks of preparation, all for this moment.

Kyle waved her through and pointed to the empty work shed. 'Bring it straight inside.' She parked it up and Kyle pulled the shed's massive sliding doors shut, blocking out the sun. '*Lock the front gate, JT.*'

'Why are we locked in?' Kat asked as Kyle helped her with the driver's door.

'We don't want anyone to accidentally tell Frank what we're doing to his ute.'

'Good point.' The Beast was famous for being Uncle Frank's chariot of choice.

'So, how are you?'

'I'm okay.' She'd done her best to avoid any one-on-one time with the guy this past week, preferring he'd use the time to build a relationship with their daughter.

'*Food!* I can smell it from here.' Jimmy loped over and

grabbed Kat in a ground-lifting bear hug.

'Put me down.'

'Humph. You bring me food, woman?' Jimmy grunted, giving his best caveman impersonation.

'Now I know why your son grunts, and I can't feed you if you don't put me down.'

'Good point.' Jimmy grinned as he messed up her hair like her head was a cut orange on a handheld juicer. 'How's my niece?'

Why did he always do that? She swiped Jimmy's big hands away as she tried to tidy up her hair. 'Kaytlyn's good, she's with her cousins and Aunty Nora at Wendy's place preparing for a slumber party.' Kaytlyn loved having an extended family. A luxury Kat never had, but would never deny her daughter, who'd coped a thousand times better than Kat with this whole situation.

'So, what've we got?' Jimmy rubbed his hands together, peeking into the ute's cab.

Kat pulled out a large platter and carried it to the back, where Kyle lowered the tray's rear door to create a serving table. 'Roast lamb shanks, and that green stuff on the side, that's called salad.' She smiled, aware lamb was Jimmy's favourite, and a rarity because very few sheep survived the Northern Territory climate.

'Your uncle trained you well, Kit-Kat. Gawd, it's still hot,' mumbled Jimmy with a mouthful, gripping the bone and looking every part the caveman.

'What's the plan?' Kat asked Kyle.

'I'll explain while we eat lunch, if you're willing to listen to what I say?'

'Told you, I can take directions.' For work, yes, her private life, no.

Hours later, inside the mechanics shed, Kat, with a mask, goggles, and oversized overalls, played with the electric sander. Music blasted in her ears as she sanded down the driver's door.

'OOH BABY I—' Kat stopped singing, as she shook the sander that had stopped working. 'What the—' She turned around to find Kyle holding the separated power cords, laughing at her. She pulled out her blaring earphones. 'Hey, I was getting into that.'

He smirked at her as he rolled up the extension cord to the bench. 'Don't quit your day job for a singing career, okay.'

'I've heard your singing too, mate, and I don't see any recording contracts covering your office desk.' His laugh made her smile with a warmth inside her chest, but she was only here for one reason. 'What do we do now?'

Kyle glided his palm over the sides of the ute. 'Now that you've sanded back enough, I'll apply the primer. Good job, by the way.'

'Thanks.' She grinned, feeling pride dust her shoulders.

The shed around her was closed up. The lights were on,

but the windows were dark. 'Where's Jimmy and JT?'

'Gone home for the night.'

'Why, what's the time?' She lifted her goggles higher and searched for the wall clock. 'Seven o'clock.' Time had just flown.

Kyle, with air hose in hand, blew all the sawdust off the vehicle, including herself, as he laughed.

'*Prick!*' She called out against the strong air jets dusting her off. At least it was cooling.

'Couldn't resist it. You should see yourself.'

'I'm not dressed to impress,' she replied, windblown and grimy from the work.

He winked at her as he lowered his own face mask and started spray painting the grey primer on the Beast.

So far, the preparations had taken the longest, taping windows and handles before they could paint, but now she watched the old ute being magically transformed.

Kyle stopped and beckoned to her with his crooked finger. 'Want to have a go?'

'You bet.' She put on her mask and skipped over. He stood behind her, his arm over her shoulder and taught her how to spray paint. At first, it was hard to concentrate with him holding her, but she soon learned, and then it was done. 'Now what?'

Kyle rolled up the air hose and switched on the large industrial fans, set on the corners of the now grey ute. 'Let it dry for a bit, then you can give it a light re-sanding before I apply the next coat. We'll let it set for the night, then I'll do another coat in the morning.'

'Will we finish it this weekend?'

'Should do, the Territory weather is perfect for drying paint.' He cleaned out the spray gun and turned the noisy compressors off, leaving the whirling fans to guard the Beast in the centre of the work shed.

'Come on, let's see if those boys left us any food in the office.'

She clopped behind him and slipped off JT's spare gumboots that were ten sizes too big. Leaving them at the door, she followed Kyle into the cool air-conditioned office.

It was a big broom closet with bare off-white walls, white tiled floor with boxes stacked in the corner and a desk covered in paperwork. The couch was cool but the spare spot irritated her. She tapped on the wall above her head as she plonked onto the couch, before her was the tray of leftovers sitting on the small coffee table. 'You need a picture here.'

'I have the perfect one.'

'No, you're not?'

'Well, you won't accept my painting.'

'It's not that I don't want it, but...' She pointed to the wall and raised her eyebrow. 'Actually, it'll be perfect there. *But,* I'll only let you hang it here *if* you let me do up this blokey broom closet.' *If she found the time.* But she also wanted to repay him for all the work he was doing on the Beast.

'Done.' He picked up the platter and held it out to her.

'Thanks.' Grabbing some food, she asked, 'How come you don't spray paint cars anymore?'

'You need a spray booth, which I don't have and haven't needed to make one. We're busy enough working on engines.'

'So, business is good?'

'I've got no more bank loans and have a steady stream of customers from this town and the neighbouring towns, too.'

'Words out, huh?'

'I'm lucky I've got a great team and my brother helping me out. It must have been hard for you, bringing up Kaytlyn on your own.'

'I manage. Like you, we cope.' She shrugged and sat quietly, but his intense stare was scaring her. Her insides were tingling ferociously, it was almost irresistible, and she needed air. 'I might see if that…' She went to open the door, but he jumped up behind her and pushed it shut.

'Why do you keep running away from me?' His warm breath tickled her ear as his familiar salty, citrus-spiced aroma wove around her like a comforting, invisible blanket.

'I'm not running away, I wanted to check on the Beast.' But he still had her trapped inside.

'You've been doing this to me for as long as I've known you,' he whispered, as his other hand stroked her hair. 'Every year you did this, and you've been avoiding me all week.'

'Have not.'

He arched his eyebrow at her; he was right.

'You and Kaytlyn needed time together,' she said.

'I'm grateful for that, but I don't want to push you away either.'

'You haven't pushed me away.'

'Not like you do with me.'

'What are you talking about?'

'I don't just want Kaytlyn in my life, I want you to be a part of it, too.' He turned her around to face him. 'I want *us* as well, you and me.'

'Hold on, you've just broken up with Emelia, found out you've got a daughter, and now you want more?'

'Of course, I want more.'

'Not when it'll be a rebound relationship, with you playing your part of what's expected and what a six-year-old child wants.' It's what others had whispered about with his love child appearing, and it was like everyone was waiting for them to start playing happy families.

Bah! Happy families were a fairy tale.

*   *   *

'That's not what I mean. Come on, let me explain.' He brought her back to the couch, cleared off the coffee table and sat right in front of her. 'This isn't a rebound, Kathryn. Sure, I broke up with Emelia the same day I kissed you, but for the past two months, I was supposed to propose.'

'So, the rumours were true?'

'The night of the paint party, when I saw you and Emelia

together, I couldn't keep it up and was planning to break up with her that same night. Unfortunately, it never happened, but I made sure I ended it the same day I kissed you.'

'We shouldn't have—'

'We did. That's why I told Emelia, as soon as I could, that it was over because we'd both feel guilty, and I didn't want that for us. I broke it off with Emelia because I don't love her.'

'You must've felt something for her?'

'No. She was a habit, and a woman who didn't want children. I was settling for second best. I knew that from the first moment I laid eyes on you when you strolled into this yard. This was before I'd kissed you and before I knew about Kaytlyn. It was you.' He reached out and held her hands in the space between them. 'You probably don't want to hear this, and I've never told you before, and I've been kicking myself for not telling you sooner.'

'Tell me what?'

He had to tell her. 'That I have loved you for as long as I can remember.'

'But—'

'No buts, just hear me out. You've always said we were a romance that only lasted as long as the summer, but we'd always be friends.'

'Those were the rules,' she whispered.

'I hated those rules, I only did it for you. Remember our last summer together, I told you I loved you every day before you returned to college? I'd asked you to stay and marry me, so we'd be together forever. That was the last night we lay in that red ute's rear tray, where—for the first time—you admitted you loved me. Do you remember?'

'I remember.'

'You picked that argument with me on purpose that night too.'

'I did not.'

'Yes, you did. It's what you always do, and I bet you don't know why.'

'Go on smart arse, the couch is here. Do you want me to lie down and have me tell you all? Do you charge by the hour?'

He chuckled at her sass—it was damned sexy on her. 'Because of what your mother and stepfather did to you as a child, you have this built-in fear of rejection. It's why you were always pushing me away at the end of every summer, to protect yourself. I get that. It's why you warned me to never do that to Kaytlyn, too. I promised Kaytlyn I wouldn't do that to her and I promise you I'll never do that to you. *Never.*'

'B-b-but,' she stammered, with tears forming in her eyes. It broke his heart.

He stroked her cheek to try and soothe them both. 'Let me finish, please?' He had to finish this, before any more of life's distractions got in the way, not when he'd finally found his voice.

She nodded, and he squeezed her hands gently.

'That last summer, it was six weeks after you left, I decided to go and see you. It took me two weeks to plan and get the time off, because I was going to ask you something, but I never made it.'

'That's when you had that accident?'

He nodded. 'And then you'd left the state. If I hadn't had that accident, things may have been different between us, because I was coming to see you.'

'You were?'

'Six months later, when I'd returned to work, I found all of your phone messages. That's when I tried to contact you, but you'd gone. Your Uncle Frank and Aunty Bea didn't know where you were, they told me you'd dropped out of art college and disappeared. Then you rang them three years later, I remember the day.'

'How?'

'Frank came and saw me here.'

'He did?'

'Yep, I'd used my insurance money from the accident to buy this place and was living in the caravan out the back, when Frank showed up with a meat tray. He said he'd won it at the pub, along with a slab of beer. Of course, he kept the Beast parked on the street, while we had a barbecue and drank a few beers. That's when I told him how much you meant to me, and why I was driving that night of the accident. I was coming to see you.'

'Why did you drive down?'

'I wanted to ask you something.'

'You could've just rung me, then you wouldn't have got

hurt.'

'I needed to ask you in person.'

'Why?'

'I wanted to give you something.' From the bottom of his desk drawer, Kyle pulled out a small black box, opened the lid and showed her. 'This.'

She gasped, pulling back, but he still held her hand so she couldn't bolt on him.

'I had this ring specially made for you over seven years ago when I was going to ask you to marry me. Sure, we were young, but I would've waited until you were ready. I had my trade certificate, which was my ticket to work anywhere, and I wanted to support you while you finished art college. I didn't care where we ended up because I didn't want to live apart from you anymore. That's why I drove down that night.'

Her eyes flickered from the ring to him, then back to the diamond.

'Even though it's seven years later, I still want to marry you, Kathryn, and I'm not letting you run away again, not without me.'

'What are you saying?'

'If you and Kaytlyn move, I'll go with you.'

'But you love it here.'

'I love you too much to not have you in my life. I'm not asking because of Kaytlyn, or because it's the right thing to do. It's because I still feel the same way about you, if not more than I did back then. If there hadn't been a car accident, who knows, we may have been married. Or at least, you wouldn't have suffered on your own, when you first found out you were pregnant. I wanted to marry you before you were pregnant.' With his fingertip, he lifted her chin to make her face him, and saw the overwhelming emotions swimming in her eyes.

'I'm not expecting you to answer my question straight away,' he said, 'because you won't. Just know that, if you do want to marry me, all you have to do is say the word. I'm not going anywhere, and I don't want any more rules if you do, okay?' She needed time; he knew that about her.

She whispered with hunched shoulders. 'But there's, er, what with my uncle's condition, Aunt Bea, my da—our daughter, they come first.'

'I know they do.' And he was nowhere on her list.

At least she'd heard him out.

'Now we can apply another coat of primer,' he said. 'I'll drop you off home after that, and then I will leave you alone.'

'What? You're—'

'I'll be leaving you alone. It's what you want.' He put the ring back into the drawer, not expecting her to say yes tonight, or ever. But he was not letting fate take away his chances again, not without her knowing everything. It was up to Kat now.

He led her back into the shed to finish the last task that tied them together, because he was worried once the ute was done, she'd be done with him too.

Twenty-Three

Kat couldn't sleep. Kaytlyn was at her slumber party and Aunty Bea was playing bridge in Pine Creek. Which left Kat alone in a silent house that wasn't offering any comfort to the racing thoughts that plagued her.

Sick of staring at the walls and tossing and turning in bed, she walked the dark, deserted streets of the tiny Territorian town.

Since she'd been back, she'd revisited many of her favourite old hiking trails, walking with Kaytlyn, they'd explored the tracks around the town to watch the expansive sunsets stretch across the outback.

She craned her neck back at the night sky. It was breathtaking how big it was, with its endless galaxies of bright stars shimmering in their velvet blanket that draped above her, illuminating the way.

The small bush hospital's lights glowed ahead as a cold shiver squirrelled down her spine. She didn't care if it was out of visiting hours; she had a sudden need to check on her uncle.

She used the night code for the keypad, slid past the opening doors and down the corridor where the TV was on low in the nurses' station. But there was no one around.

As she got closer to Uncle Frank's room, she heard voices, and when she turned the corner, his room was lit up and he was in the middle of pandemonium. Nurses were working over him as machine alarms were screaming, with Stewart at the centre of it all, yelling out instructions.

'What's wrong with him?' Kat cried out from the doorway.

Stewart scowled at her. 'Nurse, get her out of here.'

'Kat, you can't be here,' said Jenny, guiding Kat back into the hallway. 'You'll have to wait here.'

'But—'

Jenny closed the doors that muffled the voices and silenced the alarm on Uncle Frank's machines.

Kat crouched on the floor with her back to the wall, hugging her daypack, watching the door, willing it to open with good news.

After a long drawn out decade of chewing her nails, the door finally opened and she jumped to her feet.

Stewart came out and said, 'Okay, he's stable.'

'What happened?'

'Your uncle suffered a slight heart failure and we had to resuscitate him. What are you doing here?'

'I don't know.' She peeked over Stewart's shoulder,

itching to get into that room. 'Is he okay now?'

Stewart touched her shoulder. 'Kat, all we can do is monitor him for now and make him comfortable. He's gone into a coma, but he is stable. For now.'

'I want to stay. Please? I won't be a nuisance. I don't want him to be alone.' She pleaded with tears blurring her vision.

'I'm sorry—'

'I will not let my uncle die alone!' Her words echoed down the corridors of the hospital where a few patients were peeking out from their rooms.

Stewart nodded. 'Okay—'

Before he'd finished his sentence, she'd rushed past him to her uncle's bedside. 'Hey, Uncle Frank, it's me, Kat.' She kissed his forehead where his face was hidden by a mask, as tubes and machines hissed and beeped around him. She hiccupped her stifled cries, scrubbing her tears away. It wasn't his time. Not yet. She wasn't ready.

She dragged the large guest chair to his bedside and sandwiched his cold, frail hand between her palms. 'I've come to crash your party if that's okay with you. So you, kind sir, have the pleasure of my annoying company for the night. Sure, the doctor will tell me you need your rest, so you sleep and I—for once—get to do all the talking.' And she talked.

She talked of Kaytlyn. She talked of what she'd do to that room he was stuck in, if she was allowed free rein to decorate with an unlimited budget. She gossiped about people he'd never met, in a building she used to live in. She told him about the eccentricities of people she passed on the city streets that used to amuse her. She whined over some of her past clients who had all the money in the world but lacked everything in taste. She even confessed her secret jealously over the mothers who had the house, the car, and the husband, at Kaytlyn's old school. She talked as she watched the sunrise through his small window. She told him of her dreams, about Kyle, and all those thoughts that plagued her, all while holding Uncle Frank's hand. She refused to leave him to die alone.

Twenty-four

From that morning on, Aunty Bea took the day shift, and Kat took the night shift, keeping a bedside vigil on Uncle Frank. Kat was determined to never leave him alone.

Word soon spread, and they came…

The *retired Knights of the round card table* came and played cards over Uncle Frank's bed, as they sipped coffee and bitched about the weather and politics.

The elderly women from the botanical society brought in fresh scones and complained about a certain water buffalo eating all of their flowers.

The Flynn brothers sat and talked about hardware and the feedstore specials, before arguing over what movies they wanted in their movie marathon that was never going to happen.

The hairdresser and her staff gave manicures and haircuts while talking about dragon fruit and mangoes.

The Kimble's brought in their whole tribe to show off

their new baby girl.

Road-train drivers talked about carting cattle to the rail yards and road conditions.

The Police arrived and asked for advice on how best to tie-up a flower-eating water buffalo to the side of their police car.

Park Rangers came and talked about quoll counts and crocodile cages.

Farmers came and talked of crops and the weather.

Fishermen came with an assortment of lures, pleading for the coordinates to his sacred fishing spots.

The entire Elsie Creek bush school drew pictures of the Beast for his wall and sang songs that filtered throughout the hospital's corridors.

Cattlemen, with their dusty jeans and sweat-stained Akubra's, came in off cattle stations, where their bootsteps echoed down the corridors.

Men from the local mine, in their fluro vests and tired eyes, visited between shifts.

Construction workers, in their high-vis gear, laced boots, and deep suntans, visited.

And they all came. Some for five minutes, others for five hours. All sharing stories of their time of knowing Uncle Frank. Some told him to wake up and have another beer with them. Some booked in jobs or asked for advice to repair things, while others spoke of their fishing adventures shared together.

But they all came to say goodbye to an old mate.

Kat still managed to take care of Kaytlyn, the house repairs, and all the other matters during the day. She brought Kaytlyn with her in the late afternoon to read to her Poppy Frank. Aunty Bea would then take Kaytlyn home to bed. After Kyle tucked in Kaytlyn and she'd fallen asleep, he came and stayed with Kat, where they both sat watching over Uncle Frank throughout the night.

Everyone in the small town of Elsie Creek made sure her Uncle Frank was never alone.

It was mid-morning when the phone rang in Aunty Bea's bright kitchen. Kat froze in her seat, fearing the worst every time it rang. Sprawled over the kitchen table before her, was the proposal for the nurses' quarters she'd been working on. She'd spent hours talking with Jenny at the hospital over this project. It's what Kat did while sitting with Uncle Frank until she fell asleep holding his big hand. She worked on her website, answered queries and talked with Kyle, where they'd even included Uncle Frank in their conversations. They never talked in depth of their future, not while she was so focused on Uncle Frank and what little time they had left together.

She swallowed hard at the thick lump in her throat and snatched up the ringing phone. Her fingers trembled so hard, making it a mission to press the receive button. 'H-hello.'

'*Frank's awake,*' cried Aunt Bea.

'He is?' Was she hearing right?

'Yes, and he's asking for you.'

'I'm—I'm on my way.'

'I'll tell him.'

She stared at the silent phone for a moment. The good news was unexpected.

But she wasn't wasting time.

She snatched up her daypack, dashed out the door, and headed for the well-worn track that led from the back of the house, through the paddock, and towards the hospital.

Kat burst through the doorway to find Uncle Frank awake and sitting upright in bed with a tray of food in front of him. His room was full of rich aromatic flowers, boxes of beer, and assorted fishing gear, all from the townspeople. Cards covered the shelves, while pictures from children covered the walls.

'Hey, how are you?' Kat asked as she approached his bedside.

'Honestly, kiddo, I feel like an unbranded mob of mongrel bulls have charged me for entrée, then I got rolled by a flamin' road train for main course.' Uncle Frank shared a tired smile, but a spark was in his eyes. He held out his hand, and she grabbed it as he pulled her to take a seat in the chair on the other side of the bed, opposite Aunty Bea. 'Now, how are you doin'?'

'Good.' She shrugged, unwilling to burden the poor man.

'Bea told me you've been campin' out in my room at

nights, huh?'

'I didn't want you to be alone.'

'Like I don't want you to be alone either, kiddo,' Uncle Frank said, patting her hand.

'I'm fine, I've got Kaytlyn and there's Aunty Bea.'

'Not talking about them—I know.'

'Know what?'

'It's your greatest fear.'

'What is?' *Besides rejection.*

'Your fear of being alone.'

'Er, no, it's not.'

'Are you gonna argue with me?'

She shrugged hesitantly. Was he right?

'You made sure I wasn't alone, and you make sure Aunty Bea and Kaytlyn aren't alone, because you take care of them too. But you haven't let someone help you or be there for you, to share it with you.'

'I'm okay.'

Uncle Frank pushed up his glasses and tapped the side of his forehead. 'I remember.'

'Remember what?'

'I remember that night I was lying here, I couldn't feel anything, I couldn't move, but I could hear you.'

'You could? The night I rambled on?' *O-oh.*

'I heard you, and I heard some of the others rabbiting on too, but I heard you the clearest, kiddo.'

She sat back with wide eyes, but he refused to let go of

her hand. She'd spilled secrets that night, things she'd never told a soul.

'Now, one of the main reasons I had your Aunty Bea call you interstate, was because I'm a selfish old dog who wanted you to come home.'

'I'm here now.'

'To stay.'

She bit on her tongue to not speak, to not gasp, or dare search for the nearest exit.

'Now, the Beast and that house, it's yours. Bea and I've discussed this and we're giving it to you, for you and Kaytlyn to live in as your *home*.'

'Woah-woah. Wait up. You can't do that, it's yours and Aunty Bea's.' The man wasn't dead yet.

'No kiddo, it's yours. *Today*.'

'Aunty Bea, talk some sense into him.' The man wasn't making any sense.

'It's what we want for you. Besides, I'm getting my granny flat out the back.'

'Why? When you live in a perfectly good three-bedroom, two-bathroom house, with an indoor laundry. Did I just sound like a real estate agent?'

'I'm getting sick of the stairs,' said Aunty Bea. 'So, your Uncle Frank and I want you to live in the house, to have your own space, and do it up however you want.'

'But...' Kat winced at her aunt and uncle, both nodding at her with expressions that told her she couldn't barter her way out. *Was this real?* 'Are you sure?'

'Yes. I want this, Kathryn,' said Aunty Bea.

'We've had the plans all drawn up for Bea's unit. My design, of course,' he said, patting his thin chest. 'I've lined up the best building contractor, who's been given the green light to build.'

'When?'

'Once the Flynn brothers have survived their self-induced heart attack—'

'What?'

'I got them to order the materials for the builder to start at the end of next week. They reckon it'll take 'em a week. The construction crew'll be stayin' at the pub, so that'll be good business for the town. It's what my Bea wants and so do I. You'll also be project managing the job, kiddo, which I know you can do with your eyes closed. I'll still be here to consult from my office,' he said, throwing his thumb to the wall behind his bed.

'But, so soon?'

Uncle Frank sighed, patting her hand. 'We've been planning all of this soon after we found out the treatments weren't working. My Bea's always wanted us to move into something smaller, to retire in, we just ran out of time.'

'But you love that house,' Kat said to her uncle.

'I do.'

'Me too,' said Aunty Bea. 'So now it's your turn. I'll still be there for you and Kaytlyn, but it'll be your home, too.'

'We want you living in that house the way it's meant to be, like a home,' said Uncle Frank.

'We are now.'

'But with you, kiddo, it could be here today, gone tomorrow, and whichever way the dust devil dances. You deserve better and this town can help you.'

'I don't need help, I'm fine.'

'Everyone needs help, kiddo. It took a long, hard lesson for me to learn that one.'

'Is that why you're always helping others?'

'I make a point of it. It's why this town is so special; the people here aren't afraid to help others. It's why Bea and I've always stayed here. We could've lived anywhere, but we chose Elsie Creek.'

'Because of the fishing.'

'The people. From the cranky old buggers I play cards with in the hardware store—now, what's that name you called them blokes?'

'Um.' She squeezed her lips together, feeling like a kid all over again. 'The retired knights of the round card table…' She then winced as she said, 'The outback mafia.'

'Huh, they'd get a kick hearing that. You know I'm one of 'em?'

'The Flynn brothers told me you had a chair.'

'I do. I enjoy watching those guys argue, while I also get to answer the queries of the many who visit the hardware store, on how to fix their homes. I still chuckle at the Flynn brothers shooing away that water buffalo from their new shipment of flowers.'

'We'd better make sure Cecil doesn't find this room,' Aunty Bea said, pointing at the flowers crammed on the side tables, vying for attention.

'Let the buffalo eat 'em. He's a good sort, and another reason I love this town.'

'Is it true they drink scotch while playing cards?' Kat asked.

'Er…' Uncle Frank winced, giving his wife a fleeting sideways glance. 'Bea was telling me Mrs Sternston's keen for you to run craft classes and maybe even work part-time in her store?'

Nice change of subject, Uncle.

'The window display is amazing, the whole town's still talking about it,' said Aunty Bea. 'They can't wait to see what you'll do for Christmas.'

'I only did Mrs Sternston's window to help her business. If I'm not careful, I'll probably end up buying more craft stuff from her store than I'll earn in wages.'

Uncle Frank sat taller in his bed, pushing his spectacles higher along his nose. Colour flushed in his cheeks as if he was waking up even more. 'I also want you to turn the shed's side storeroom into that big fancy office studio you told me about that night.'

'No, I didn't.'

'I heard you, kiddo. Now, there's plenty of room in there

to use as a studio.'

'Then you would've also heard me tell you what I'd do with this room with an unlimited budget.' Kat waved her hands around the hospital room that resembled a preschooler's rec room, full of drawings of rainbows, butterflies, and twenty different versions of his red ute.

'I did, and I think it's about time you got all that material out of them boxes in that storage unit. There's plenty of space in the shed on the far side.'

'That's for Aunty Bea's car.'

'I'm getting a carport for my new granny flat,' said Aunty Bea. 'So, that side's all free.'

'See.' Uncle Frank arched his eyebrow at Kat. 'You'll still be able to keep the workshop and bar in the amazing condition you have it now. Think about it, kiddo, you'll never have to pay rent again.'

'But… But…You were asleep when I told you all that stuff.' She'd confessed everything to him that night, all those secrets she'd kept bottled up for years.

'You need to tell him,' he said, patting her hand.

'Who?'

'Kyle. You need to tell him how you feel about him, too.'

'But Uncle—'

He held up his hand like a traffic sign. 'Ah, lemme finish. The other reason I asked you to come back was for that boy, Kyle.'

She frowned, asking warily, 'Why?'

'When I heard Kyle was going to ask someone else to marry him, he was doing it for all the wrong reasons. Not when Kyle loves you with all his heart, and he always has, that boy. I should know, it's the same way I've always felt about my Bea, where every day I'm grateful for what time I got to spend with her.' Uncle Frank patted Aunty Bea's hand as she smiled at her husband, then he pointed at Kat. 'Yet, you're denying yourself your own happiness, kiddo. Too scared to take that chance. Now, it's my turn to confess something.' He shifted in his seat and coughed as the pair of women instantly rose to help him.

'I'm all right, I'm not gone yet.' He swatted away their hands and took a sip of water offered to him by his wife. 'Listen, kiddo, I brought you up here, not just for me, but for you too.'

'What do you mean, Uncle?'

'It was the only way to get you here—not that my Bea or anyone else knows of my cunning ways, but I'd hoped, with you being back, getting the Beast serviced straight away—'

'You didn't.' She gasped at Uncle Frank. *Was this all one big setup?*

'Then, maybe, you two could work things out.' He chuckled for a bit, that started a rattling cough until he caught his breath, but he wouldn't let her help, nor did he let go of her hand. 'Did you know Kyle was driving down to ask you to marry him? Like he's asked you again.'

'How did you know that?'

'I heard that boy talkin' to me in my sleep too. Now, I know you're scared, kiddo. Hey, I've been there myself all them years ago, not knowing if Bea would marry me. But she did, and I have lived a life of no regrets when I was so close to going the other way. Now it's your turn. You deserve to be happy and you need to do it before it's too late. You two are made for each other, everyone knows that.' he then said, poking her shoulder, 'it's just you who refuses to let it be.'

'I don't...can't...' Kat whispered. Although Uncle Frank was right, it petrified her stomach into a solid lump of dry ice.

'How about you start one day at a time and start by opening up that beautiful loving heart you have inside. Listen, not with your head, but with your heart.' He winked at her with a grin. 'Now, gimme a hug before you go. I need a nap, and I want you to have a really good think about this. I can't decide for you, no one can, I can only tell you how I see it.'

She leaned over and hugged him; he kissed her forehead like she was that little girl all over again. She didn't want him to go.

Uncle Frank brushed her hair away and held her chin. 'I've always loved you like you were my own, and all I want is to see you happy.'

'I love you too, Uncle Frank.' She hugged him again and then hugged Aunty Bea, before she trudged to the door and glanced back at the elderly couple.

Uncle Frank sat up in his bed and gave her *the nod*. It was the same nod she got when she climbed onto the bus to leave.

At the end of every summer, she'd look over her shoulder while on the steps of the bus, and he'd nod at her as if to say, *seeya later*. It was a nod of understanding. A nod that said more than just a nod. It was goodbye.

She rushed back and gave him another big hug. 'Love you too, Uncle, and thank you,' she said as if it was for the last time.

Twenty-Five

Kat walked the tracks behind the hospital, lost in her thoughts, passing magnetic termite mounds as tall as cathedral spires. Some of the shorter ant mounds were dressed in t-shirts and sun-faded Santa hats that reminded her of the Swedish tomte dolls of Christmas.

She walked the dusty roads guarded on either side by barbed wire fences that held cattle with horns wider than push bike handles. She passed beneath the shade of the heady scented flowering gumtrees where screeching rainbow lorikeets eagerly lapped up the nectar.

Shouldering her way through the pink-flowered turkey bush, tiny blue wildflowers brushed her boots, and she soon found herself back on the strip of black asphalt that rolled ahead like a never-ending carpet.

In the distance, she spotted the train sliding through the open landscape like a snake across the desert sand. It was heading for the tiny Territorian town of Elsie Creek that spread below her as she walked further away from town.

Clip-Clop. Clip-clop. Clip-clop.

She stopped.

The *clip-clop* stopped.

She turned and there it was, the big black water buffalo with a black shiny nose. 'Shoo.'

But it just stood there on the road, chewing like a cow, wearing yellow fluorescent ribbons hanging off its horns and tail. This time the words on the side read: *'Frank's awake!'*

'How did they know?' How long had she been walking around for?

She turned and started back down the road.

Clip-clop, clip-clop, the buffalo followed.

She stopped.

The buffalo stopped but got no closer.

'This is all too weird,' she said, with her back to the buffalo.

She took a step and stopped.

The buffalo stepped and stopped.

She took two steps and stopped.

The buffalo took two steps and stopped.

She walked, it followed. She knew she couldn't outrun a water buffalo. Instead, she giggled, as the *clip-clop, clip-clop* echoed around her, and she laughed louder, walking with the buffalo at her back.

She walked along the road with the buffalo following as Uncle Frank's questions rattled through her, most of all, could she stay here, permanently?

Kaytlyn loved it here. She loved the school, her treehouse, and the backyard. She had her best friend, finger-sucking Sammy next door, and they played with other children in the street on weekends and after school. She had her cousins, and her Aunty Nora and Uncle Jimmy, who all adored her. Most of all Kaytlyn had her father here.

But did the town have enough for Kat to stay?

If anything, she'd learned to plan. She was always making plans, if not on paper for her future artwork, it was long-term planning on income to pay for her and Kaytlyn.

Well, the house would be rent-free, which would be a huge strain off her shoulders. She had the nurses' proposal to work on. Future craft classes, monthly window dressings, and supply contracts with the hardware store.

She also had her online businesses. And, Uncle Frank's place had the perfect treasure trove of trinkets stored at the back of his shed. Not to mention a fully decked-out workshop to play with. Perhaps, she could be comfortable here.

She stopped, and the *clip-clop* stopped behind her.

She was thinking with her head and not with her heart.

So, what did her heart want?

What did she love about this place?

She craned her neck back to stare at the biggest sky in the world. She used to try and touch it on Uncle Frank's shoulders when she was a kid, and he'd swoop her up into his arms whenever she arrived on the bus.

She remembered that giddy feeling, every single year

the excitement would build, the closer she got to another summer of freedom. Free from walls and away from the confined dormitory of boarding school, hemmed inside a capital city where everyone was watching.

All of it was exchanged for dirt tracks in native scrublands. The pure joy of finding a secluded waterfall with water so clear you could see the bottom and knew it was free from crocodiles to swim in. The times she'd sat riverside or in boats and watched the majestic glide of the freshwater whiprays. How long neck turtles would pop their noses out of the water to watch her fishing. She'd smile wide, pointing, as she said, 'Did you see that?' But she wasn't speaking to Uncle Frank or Aunty Bea, it was Kyle.

It had always been Kyle who had her back. The boy who grew into the man, who consistently gave her the courage to see what was around the track's bend, to find new treasures on the path ahead.

That giddy excitement of the bus coming to town to start her holidays wasn't just for her aunt and uncle, it was to see Kyle. The letters she wrote him, wanting to share with him when she'd got an A for her sculpture, or her scholarship to design school. He'd been happy for her and had always encouraged her.

She'd shared everything with him, from her crayons and paper to draw side by side, way back then he'd only show his drawings to her. The long drives going nowhere with the windows down, the stereo blaring, where they'd sing as bad as the other. They used to dance like no one cared, celebrating the joy of summer rain on the desert sand.

They'd laid in the back of the Beast and shared all their dreams and secrets, staring at the sea of stars in a never-ending skyline. The comfortable silences shared on their outback treks of discovery, and how they'd stare at each other after having made love, where his eyes spoke straight to her soul.

Kyle was the one who'd always soothed her fears of failure. The one she'd run to whenever she got scared, like the day she'd destroyed the letterbox, denting the Beast.

Even all these years apart, she'd thought about him when she'd see something on the street he'd appreciate, or those first precious moments of their daughter's life.

Had she really been denying him his happiness?

Was she denying herself—in the only place that truly felt like home?

Why was she so scared of taking that risk, that first step, why?

Was love enough to live happily forever?

Again, the fear of rejection squeezed that familiar knot in her stomach, the one she'd been living with for so long. Again, she heard the question—was love enough?

She started walking, and the buffalo clip-clopped behind her.

A willy-willy danced across the wide savannah plains, stirring red dust and leaves in a jagged pattern. It crossed the road and passed in front of her, where she'd stopped with the buffalo. She watched the windstorm spin and dance across the red dirt to the tarmac. Then it disappeared and the dust fell like red rain, to settle on the soil.

'Huh?' It was like the story of her life, moving in a zig-zag jagged pattern to never settle, always keeping busy, renovating her apartments at all hours of the night so she never knew how lonely she was. It's why she was always fixing things, fixing Uncle Frank's house, his car, the kitchen sink, because she wanted to fix her past. A past she couldn't fix, nor the man. Most of all, she'd kept herself busy so she didn't miss what her heart desired the most. Kyle.

Her uncle was right, life was precious, and she didn't want to die unhappy, or alone—not without taking that chance.

She stared at the road ahead that stretched out like a black carpet, rolling off into the unseen infinity, as if it was her future. She remembered staring at that same road when she had first returned to Elsie Creek, carrying all those feelings of dread, guilt, rejection and history. But now, it was a blank canvas before her, and she was no longer scared.

She turned and faced the buffalo that had frightened her when they'd first arrived back in town. 'Cecil, is it?'

It raised its big head, and with its shiny black nose, he began sniffing at her backpack. She pulled off her simple daypack that carried the essentials, like water, hat, sunscreen, insect repellent, and some trail mix and muesli bars. In the bottom was a spare packet of Kaytlyn's coloured chalk they'd used to mark their trails on their afternoon walks.

An idea hit and she grinned at the buffalo sniffing at the muesli bars, the one Kaytlyn said the buffalo favoured.

'I need your help, Cecil. I'll give you half now, and half later.' She cracked open the muesli bar and hand fed it to the buffalo. It was the strangest sensation, those velvet lips against her hand and his warm breath. She couldn't believe she was doing such a thing.

'I have an idea, Cecil. I just hope we're not too late?'

* * *

Kat walked with the muesli bar held out in her hand as the buffalo followed, taking the back roads into town. Cars tooted as they passed her, with their drivers waving and yelling out congratulations on her Uncle Frank being awake.

She waved back as she kept coaxing Cecil, hoping this would work. She'd been a fool for long enough.

They stopped in front of the mechanics shop, and in the centre stood Uncle Frank's ute, fully restored. The Beast was now a fiery red, with shiny new hubcaps and whitewall tyres, sparkling in the sun. It looked brand new.

The gravel crunched under her boots as she stared at her distorted reflection in the high gloss polish of the panels. It was immaculate.

'Have you come for the ute?' Kyle asked, coming up

behind her.

'It looks fantastic.' All those past scratches, the faded paint, the life and stories it had in its dents, were all gone. The Beast had been given a second chance to start a whole new chapter in its life.

'I see you brought a friend.' Kyle pointed to the buffalo plucking at some weeds by the front gate. 'I'm surprised you're not screaming and running away from him.'

'My stalker and I have come to an agreement.'

He pointed to the words blazoned on the buffalo's side. 'Hey, is Frank really awake?'

'Awake and talking.'

'Good.' He sighed with relief. 'How are you?'

'Um...' She stared into his intense blue eyes that warmed her soul, and his sly-tequila smile she thirsted for. Kyle had always held an inner strength that matched his sensitivity she admired. 'Can I ask you a question?'

'Anything.'

'Great, wait there.' She dumped her pack in the dirt and grabbed the last muesli packet from her pocket. 'Come on, Cecil, it's showtime.' She turned him around to show the other side where she'd drawn in chalk...

Move in with me?

'What the—' Kyle's jaw dropped and then he frowned.

'So, um, that's me asking you to move in with me.' Was she too late?

'Huh?'

She licked her lips and held her breath, as if she stood on the edge of the escarpment, about to dive into the bottomless tropical waterfall. 'Kyle, I'm asking.'

'Are you kidding me?' His frown deepened, tilting his head as if to listen harder. 'You wrote that on the side of a buffalo? What's the catch? Do you want me to sleep on the couch? To stay friends where I'm not allowed to touch you like you said at the paint party?'

'No, I didn't mean it like that. You'll be with me.'

'For how long? Until the end of next summer?'

'I-I-I...' It was time to take that leap into the future and let others help her. Kyle had done that with her, for her, even when she didn't want it, he'd been there. He was right, her rules kept him back to protect herself, when it was her own rules that were hurting her the most.

Leaving Cecil to scavenge some flowering weeds along the fence line, she approached Kyle. 'I had to get your attention and tell you I'm sorry. Will you hear me out?'

He crossed his arms over his chest. 'Why? You gonna give me a stack of rules to go with that proposal?'

'No.'

'All right, I'm listening.'

He wasn't happy, and it was all her fault. Now she had to fix it. 'I'm sorry for pushing you away. I'm sorry for being this idiot making up all those stupid rules for you. I'm sorry I didn't try hard enough to include you in our daughter's life, and for not reaching out every year. I'm sorry for being so busy, not realising that the most precious person I had in the world, wasn't just my daughter, but her father, who is my best friend and my one true love. Can you ever forgive me for my stupidity, especially for trying to fix my past by pushing you away, when what I really want is a future, with you.'

With arms crossed over his chest, his intense eyes narrowed at her. 'No.'

'What?' Her heart dropped and her whole body wanted to fall with it.

Kyle stepped in so close his salty citrus-spiced aroma wrapped around her. She didn't want to lose that scent or the man. 'You know what I want, you've heard my offer.'

It was time to let go. To brush off the past scratches and dents, and to put on a new coat of paint and face the future for the long-term. 'Do you still want to ask me, I mean, I'd understand because I blew it—'

He held her upper arms and lowered himself where his blue eyes with the gold flecks spoke directly to her soul. 'Are you ready for me to ask?'

Even if her stomach was swirling with its own cyclonic storm, she was ready and believed it. 'Now. Ask me now. Here.'

'Stay right there.' Kyle ran into the shed and into his office.

'Oi, where's the fire?' yelled Jimmy, popping his head out from beneath a car bonnet.

'Stay there,' Kyle called out as he ran back to Kat,

standing by the Beast.

'What's going on?' JT asked, popping his head up from another car. He walked over to stand beside Jimmy, both looking out to the yard. 'They're not gonna do that kissing thing again, are they?'

'Why? Reckon you can handle another round or are you still shell-shocked from last time?' Jimmy laughed at the lad next to him.

'Yeah-nah.' JT frowned. 'Hey, I wanna hear what she thinks of the whitewall tyres—' JT started to move but Jimmy put his big paw on JT's scrawny shoulder.

'You heard the boss, we wait.'

'I have waited too long to do this.' Kyle wiped his palms across his t-shirt, got down on one knee in the middle of the mechanics yard, and held out the opened jeweller's box to Kat.

'Oh man, he's—' JT froze with wide eyes.

'Proposing,' said Jimmy.

Clip-crunch. The buffalo's hooves crunched into the gravel as he crossed the driveway, sniffing the air towards Kat and Kyle.

'Quick, stop Cecil from butting in,' Jimmy said to JT. They dashed across the yard to cut off the water buffalo and held it back by the horns. 'You can carry on now,' Jimmy said to his little brother.

'Well, I'm not waiting any longer. Kat—Kathryn…' Kyle reached for her hand and held the ring to the tip of her finger while he remained on bended knee.

'You don't have to do this,' she said to Kyle.

'Ah, I want to do this properly. Considering you've put your art on the side of a buffalo, I'm hoping to outdo it.' He cleared his throat and said, 'Kathryn Jones, since the moment you drove back into this yard with that backfiring, rust bucket of a beast.' He nodded to the now polished car beside her. 'Not only are you the love of my life, you are also my muse. You were my summer of spontaneous, mapless days, with your freckles, your watermelon smiles, and ice-cream sticky fingers. You had this gift of turning down the drama of my day with your smile, which always sang loudly to my soul.' He grabbed her hands and stared up at her from bended knee. 'You are the colour behind my closed eyelids, the summer sun flare to my dark, and the wild storm's passionate rain a desert would die without. Kathryn, you are everything in my world, and it'd be my greatest honour if you would become my life partner so our summer love story never ends.' Kyle gazed up at her with hope. He'd dreamed of this moment for over seven years, and now he was finally asking. 'All you have to do is say yes.'

Tears trickled down her cheeks, seeing a true love in the depth of his eyes, and knew he meant every single syllable of those beautiful words.

She nodded. 'Yes.'

'Finally!' He slipped the ring onto her finger, kissed the back of her hand, jumped to his feet and hugged her, lifting her up in his arms. He was never going to let her go.

Standing on either side of Cecil, JT and Jimmy wolf

whistled and clapped.

'So, when do you want to get married?' Kyle asked Kat.

'As soon as we can. I think we've wasted enough time, don't you?'

'I'd marry you yesterday if you'd let me.'

'Well then, you can move in with me today into our *home* and we can plan our future together.'

'Done.' He kissed her lips, rested his forehead against hers and whispered. 'I love you.'

'I LOVE YOU TOO,' she shouted to the world, and kissed the man she'd always loved.

'Yeah-nah, they're kissing again,' JT whined while hugging the water buffalo's neck. 'They're not gonna get all hot and sweaty like they did before, yeah?'

'Nah, that only happens before you get the ring on a woman's finger. It's all a ploy, you know, sex don't exist once you get married.' Jimmy roared with laughter on the other side of the buffalo, wiping happy tears from the corners of his eyes. 'We'd wanna change Cecil's sign to let the town know, otherwise, lots of people might move in with Cecil. Here, you do it.' Jimmy held out some large chunks of chalk to JT.

'Why are you walking around with chalk in your pockets?'

'The kids' rooms are painted in chalk paint. It's good fun drawing all over their walls, keeps you in touch with your inner kid.'

JT chuckled as he wrote on the side of the buffalo. One

side read, '*Frank is awake*'. On the other side, it read, '*Kat and Kyle are engaged, finally!*'

Jimmy added a love heart to the side, then patted the buffalo's rump. 'Off you go, Cecil, share the love with the world, mate.' He then faced the kissing couple with hands on his hips. 'Finally, after all these years. Man, it's good to have Kit-Kat back in town.' He messed up JT's hair, then went to congratulate the couple.

Cecil, the water buffalo, waddled out the front gate, swishing his black tail as the ribbons flapped in the breeze. He turned towards the main street where cars tooted, people waved, and the many cheers followed the walking billboard as he spread the news through the township of Elsie Creek.

Cattlemen, miners, fishermen, and farmers wandered out from the pub's front bar where they raised their beers and cheered loudly. Their united voices echoed along the main street where many came out from their stores to see what the fuss was about. Mrs Sternston and a group of women pointed and smiled at Cecil as they peeked through her new fancy shop window. The Flynn brothers, with thumbs tucked into their leather work aprons, nodded with matching grins out front of their hardware store. Nora and Wendy hugged each other as they jumped up and down while crying with joy behind the supermarket window.

As the shadows stretched across the main street, Cecil,

with ribbons waving from his horns and tail, followed the setting sun. Behind him, the people of Elsie Creek came together to celebrate, in a place where the summer never ended and where the summer sweethearts would forever call *home*.

THE END

For now...

DIAMOND IN THE DUST

MEL A ROWE

ONE

Over teeth-chattering corrugations and rocks, Verily navigated the small scooter through the treacherous terrain. Her smile grew, as the wind whipped her sun-bleached hair free from the edges of the bike helmet. It was as if she was the only person alive in this place. Inhaling clean air, zipping along the red-dirt road that contrasted with the biggest of blue skies.

Cattle, with wide handle-bar sized horns, grazed in the wide-open paddock. Across the road, rows of barren mango trees followed the curve of the land belonging to Verily's aunt.

Suddenly, the ground shook and vibrated through her seat like an earth tremor as a low earthy rumble grew to a roar behind her. Her eyes widened at the reflection in her side mirror and her heart jumped to her throat as fear spiked to an all-time high.

A devil's dust storm of explosive, churning red soil spewed high into the air. Its cause was a mountain of metal that led the tornado, and it was the biggest truck Verily had ever seen—charging straight for her.

If I can get through my Aunt's front gates, I'll be safe. Verily twisted the throttle, forcing the bike to go faster, she was trapped between two barbed wire fences that shone under the afternoon that could seriously damage skin.

The dust demon barrelled toward her. The ground shook, and the noise was horrendous.

'NOOOOO!' Her scream was lost in the deafening roar as trailers taller than houses passed by, one after the other, after the other.

The more she tried to ride through the storm, the more it dragged her along with the truck—straight for those towering tyres.

She hit the brakes. The bike skidded, her ears rung, and the train on wheels engulfed her in an apocalyptic world of red rain and thunder.

Buckets of gritty red powder showered over her, filling her ears and nose, crunching grit in her teeth, while her tongue was like sandpaper. It was suffocating.

Then, like a summer's monsoon, the walls of red dust fell, and the cloud moved away.

'What the hell?' Verily spat out dirt, wiping at her gritty eyes. She was completely covered, rolled, and basted in a coat of red grit.

She scowled at the mobile storm that slowed down with a hiss of its brakes. It then turned right—straight into her Aunt's place, tumbling past the main house, then down the track and disappearing into the mango orchard.

How does a truck that big, just vanish?

It wasn't any of her business, Verily was only the visitor. She was always the visitor.

Rolling her left shoulder, ignoring the dull ache, she gunned the dust-spluttering bike and slowly rolled back to Molly's, hoping to blow away the dust she wore. It was everywhere.

She steered through the thick fallen layers of dirt that had erased all other tracks on the road, it was like riding on freshly fallen snow. Everything in this place was new ground, ever since she'd returned to this country. It was a land she had once called home, yet she felt like an alien. A red dust covered alien.

Why did she come here at all? There were far better places to holiday than being stuck in the middle of the outback.

*　　*　　*

Alex steered over fifty metres of moveable metal to the centre of the mango orchard and parked the prime mover behind his cottage. It snaked around the building, shielding it from the rows of trees as the smell of cattle wafted from the empty trailers.

On the veranda, he tossed his Akubra on the hook by the back door, ripped off his long-sleeved shirt and chucked it straight into the washing machine. He dusted down his jeans by the laundry tub, and splashed water to rid the dust and dirt from his face and hair. There was no time for a shower, so the pommy powder shower would have to do, and he let the deodorant can do its worst.

He snatched a fresh shirt from the clothesline that stretched across his veranda, he took a mouthful of milk from the old beer fridge, then sighed at the sight of the bottled beer calling to his taste buds. 'Soon fellas, soon.'

He held up a label-less bottle to the afternoon light. There was minimal sediment with a promising clarity to the pale ale. Would this be his winning brew?

He spotted the clock on the wall. 'Crap, I'm late.'

Shoving the t-shirt over his head, he snatched his duffel-bag from the old armchair. Small dust clouds stirred beneath his boots as he headed for his ute and followed the dirt track that ran through the mango orchard, to Molly's house. Their stout trunks and sturdy branches were naked and ready for fruit bearing. Alex was looking forward to their flowering, hoping his new pruning technique would work on the next crop. A crop that would p

ay for his dream future.

He pulled up to Molly's stone house with its deep verandas, where he'd spent many an afternoon. The place was his second home.

In through the back door and into the large open kitchen, he grabbed the water cooler from Molly's pantry. Its shelves were stacked with jams and preservatives, and where the bickie tin called his name.

With a sweet biscuit in his mouth, Alex filled the water bottles at the sink. 'Hey, Molly, you ready?'

No answer.

He chomped on his biscuit as his boot-steps echoed along the wooden floorboards. 'Molly, you about?'

Voices carried down the corridor as he stepped through the doorway and stopped. His eyes widened, his jaw dropped, and his head tilted.

And his heart stopped, but only for a second...

Then it hammered.

Fast.

Mouth dry, it was impossible to swallow the tasteless biscuit as he stared at the heavenly vision at the end of the hallway. Long, messy sun-bleached hair. Sleepy eyes the colour of raw umber. The rest was athletically toned perfection in matching bra and bootyliscious-briefs where the word sexy just wasn't a big enough word in his vocab to define the perfection.

'WHAT THE HELL!' She screamed at him, covering herself with her arms, and dashing into the spare bedroom.

He gave a slow lopsided grin as his eyes followed that great arse through the doorway, then found himself frowning at the mash of red, angry scars that ran down her left shoulder and upper arm.

The door slammed, snapping him back to reality.

'Um, sorry,' he mumbled to the closed door. Not really. It'd been the best perve he'd had all bloody year. 'Oi, Molly? Did you finally find your magic potion and turn young again?'

'I wish,' replied Molly, coming out of her room at the far end of the corridor.

'You always look the same, except for the hair.' That changed colours and styles all the time, but Molly's warm smile never changed. 'So, ah. Who's...'—the goddess behind door number one? He pointed to the closed door.

'Verily. Remember? I told you my niece was visiting.'

'Wasn't she supposed to be here last week?'

'She got hung up. Talk about being late...' Molly tapped on the closed door and sung out, 'We'll be waiting outside, Verily.'

'Won't be a sec, Aunt Molly,' came the muffled reply from behind the door.

'Aunt Molly, huh?' Alex leaned his broad shoulder against the wall. 'It's been a long time since I've heard anyone call you that.'

'I've only got one niece,' said Molly, walking past him. 'Are you coming?'

He'd rather wait for the mystical creature to come out from behind that shut door. 'Ah, yeah.' He followed Molly and grabbed the esky and water coolers off the table.

Flicking through her vast umbrella collection from the rack he'd made her way back in school, Molly plucked a blue one that matched her dress. 'Now, do me a favour, Alex. Don't tell Verily where we're going or what we're doing.'

'Why? It's not like it's a secret. The whole town knows about it.'

Entering the kitchen in a pair of sweatpants that hung low on her hips, Verily threw her hair into a ponytail and asked, 'The whole town knows what?'

That a goddess had moved into town. She looked like someone who'd just jumped out of bed, but sexier.

'Nothing,' said Molly, pushing open the creaking flyscreen door. 'Come along, hon, we're late.'

'Sorry, I had to take a shower because some idiot in this massive truck covered me in dust. I nearly got sucked under the tyres,' Verily said, following them outside.

'Ah crap,' mumbled Alex, and headed for the safety of his ute.

'Then,' continued Verily, 'that monster tore down your driveway and disappeared into the mango orchard. How does a truck that big disappear?'

'Sorry, Molly,' said Alex, wincing at Molly raising her eyebrow at him. 'I didn't want to be late.'

'That was you?' Verily narrowed her eyes at him from the other side of the rear tray. 'You—whoever the hell you are—almost sucked me under those tyres. I almost suffocated in all that dust.'

'Were you walking, hon?' Molly asked Verily.

'No, I was having a great ride on your scooter, until I swallowed enough sand to make my own Bondi Beach.'

'No need to be so dramatic,' said Alex, shaking his head. 'I thought you were some kid who'd pinched that bike, the way you were wobbling.'

'I was learning! It's not easy riding in that powdery red dirt.'

'It's called bulldust.' Typical tourist. 'Most people pull over to let a road train pass on dirt tracks, but you were trying to outrun me. Weren't you?'

Her dainty chin lifted and her lips tightened. She was mad at him—but those bedroom eyes of hers were damned sexy.

He grinned for a moment, then matched princess-drama's frown. 'Welcome to the Territory, Princess, where red dust is part of everyone's daily diet in the dry season. Get used to it—' Or leave.

Find the rest of the story
at your favourite online bookstore...

Did you like the story?

If so, *your opinion* matters to me!

I'd love to read your review on

GOODREADS & BOOKBUB.

Or share a cover of this book on social media so I can

see how far this story has travelled!

Please add *#Escape2HEA* for me to find you.

With much gratitude,

Mel.

MelAROWE.com

Thank you!

For reading this story of the fictitious Northern Territory township of Elsie Creek. She may not exist, yet there is a part of her found in the NT townships, roadhouses, dusty sports grounds, crocodile-crowded boat ramps, and even in the hidden rural pubs sparsely scattered across northern Australia.

Thank you to the amazing Handbrake for not disowning me. Thank you to my sister for her support and for her part as the NT muse. I'm okay with the knowledge that neither of you, or anyone in my family, have ever read a word I've written, so I'm putting this right here in case you do dare to indulge.

Thank you to my writer friends I've met online who've helped me so much when I live in a world where finding decent Wi-Fi is like discovering gold. On top are the sparkling gems, my CP and my fabulous First Readers. Thank you, ladies.

Thank you to the quirky, colourful, and exceptionally extraordinary people I've met while working and living throughout the Top End of Australia. The experience has been—and continues to be—priceless.

Lastly, to you, dear reader, thank you for taking the time to read this story, where I look forward to sharing more with you in that _'Escape to Happily Ever After'_.

Thank you, because I can, because I did, and because I continue to be eternally grateful …

Until next time,

Mel A. Rowe

MelAROWE.com

About the Author

Australian Bestselling Author, Mel A ROWE, creates escapes for you to enjoy from the comfort of home.

Delivered with a dash of drama, witty humour and quirky family units, Mel is known for reinventing romantic versions of *home*, taking her common characters on uncommon journeys that lead from boardrooms to billabongs as they try to find their own HAPPILY EVER AFTER.

Living in Northern Australia, Mel enjoys random outback road trips, fumbling with her camera, annoying her family with her bad singing, and making new friends in the middle of nowhere— except for water buffalos. She's been chased by a few.

Feel free to contact Mel as her word journey continues at...

MelAROWE.com

Also by MEL A ROWE

Winter's Walk

The Football Whisperer

Avoiding the Pity Party

Unplanned Party

The Australian Bestselling
ELSIE CREEK SERIES:

The ART of DUST

DIAMOND in the DUST

CAKED in DUST

XMAS DUST

Visit MelAROWE.com for more